Jean-Baptiste Andrea was born in 1971 in Saint-Germain-en-Laye and grew up in Cannes. Formerly a director and screenwriter, he published his first novel, *Ma Reine*, in 2017. It won twelve literary prizes, including the Prix du Premier Roman and the Prix Femina des Lycéens.

Sam Taylor is an author and former correspondent for *The Observer*. His translations include Laurent Binet's *HHhH*, Leïla Slimani's *Lullaby* and Maylis de Kerangal's *The Heart*, for which he won the French-American Foundation Translation Prize.

A Hundred Million Years
and a Day

A Hundred Million Years and a Day

Jean-Baptiste Andrea

Translated from the French by Sam Taylor

Gallic Books

London

A Gallic Book

First published in France as *Cent millions d'années et un jour*
Copyright © L'Iconoclaste, 2019

English translation copyright © Sam Taylor, 2020

First published in Great Britain in 2020 by Gallic Books,
59 Ebury Street, London, SW1W 0NZ

A CIP record for this book is available from the British Library
ISBN 9781910477830
Typeset in Fournier MT by Gallic Books

Printed in the UK by CPI (CR0 4YY)

2 4 6 8 10 9 7 5 3 1

Jean-Baptiste Andrea wishes to thank
l'Istituto Culturale delle Comunità dei Ladini Storici delle Dolomiti Bellunesi
– Istituto Ladin de la Dolomites, Borca di Cadore

For my parents

Summer

I will, inevitably, forget many things, perhaps even my own name. But I will never forget my first fossil. It was a trilobite, a small marine arthropod that was peacefully minding its own business until one spring day when its existence intersected with mine. A second later, we were friends for life.

Years after this, when I was old enough to understand, the trilobite would tell me that it had survived several mass extinctions. Lava and acid, a lack of oxygen, the falling sky. And then one day it must have surrendered, recognising that its time was up, and rolled into a ball, deep within a rock. It had to accept defeat, to make way for others.

Such as me: a *Homo sapiens* in trousers that were too big for him, standing in the tall grass of a still-young century. I had been sent home from school, that morning in 1908, for telling my teacher she was wrong. Pépin was not the name of a king of France, as she claimed. It was the name of a dog, *my* dog, a blue merle Australian shepherd that we'd found in the barn. He protected us from evil spirits and stray cats – often the same thing, as everybody knew.

Mademoiselle Thiers had shown me an illustration of a small bearded man in a crown beneath the letters P-É-P-I-N. And, even though I had only just started learning to read, I had the feeling that those letters were proof that I was wrong. When she said, 'You interrupted the class, have you something to say?' I had replied: 'Next time, I'll be right.' She wrote the word *insolent* in my school notebook and underlined it twice. 'Please ask your parents to sign this.'

I walked home along the Chemin des Brousses with my twice-underlined insolence and my martyred expression. Of all the boys in the area, I was the only one who liked school, and I was the best. It was hardly my fault that the king had a dog's name, was it?

Seeing that her bedroom-window shutters were closed, I understood that I should not disturb my mother. In such moments she needed darkness, and darkness alone. The Commander was not in his usual place on the horizon, where our fields started their descent towards the village. There was only Pépin, youthful and vigilant, curled up in the wind on top of a small hill. His good ear pricked up and he glanced at me – there was indeed something kingly about him – before falling asleep again.

I grabbed a hammer, the best solution to so many of life's problems. It was better to use it far from the house, so I walked through a jungle of lettuces until a large stone stopped me in my tracks in the middle of the neighbour's field. I imagined the face of Mademoiselle Thiers on its surface and – one, two, three – dealt her a vengeful blow. The stone immediately split open, as if it had just been pretending to be whole. And, from its mineral depths, my trilobite looked me in the eye, every bit as surprised as I was.

It was three hundred million years old, and I was six.

'**D**estination?'

Last stop, I replied. The place I am heading to no longer has a name. A simple hamlet, lost at the end of a summer's day. The guy sitting under his parasol handed me a ticket and went back to sleep.

In front of me a skinny neck is tossed from side to side, threatening to snap at each bend in the road. An old woman. We are the only passengers: her, me, and an infernal heat that gets in through all the gaps – worn seals, loose screws, badly fitted windows. My forehead against the glass seeks in vain for a patch of coolness.

Umberto had not appeared by the time the shuttle left Nice so I'll have to wait for him up there. He'll catch another of these buses, with their strange white-sided tyres. He, too, will sit as it climbs for hours, feeling certain that the journey will soon be over – and he, too, will be wrong. I haven't spoken to him in a month but he'll come, I'm sure of it. He'll come because he's Umberto. And I will wait impatiently for him, cursing and ranting until he arrives, because I am me.

The neck cracks like a twig: the old woman has fallen asleep on her shopping bag. A little girl sat down with her mother a while ago, on the other side of the aisle, her legs stretched out on the red leather. I offered her the socca that I'd bought at the port – I had lost all appetite for it during those first bends. The girl stuck out her tongue, squinting at me, scorning my chickpea pancake. Her mother scolded her and I indicated that it was no big deal, even though, honestly, what a brat. Mother and daughter got off the bus maybe two hours ago, in another life. The road still unfurls ahead of us. It's true that a story often begins with a road, but I wish I knew what made mine so tortuous.

This is a land where quarrels last a thousand years. The valley deepens then meanders away, like an old person's smile. At the very end, not far from Italy, an immense cypress nails the hamlet to the mountain. The houses encircle it, jostling one another, reaching out with their hot roof tiles to touch it. The alleys are so narrow that you graze your shoulders as you walk through them. Here, space is rare and stone seeks to fill it. Man is left with almost nothing.

The village – recognisable from the photograph I'd seen, which was blurry, the ink absorbed by poor-quality paper – is like a pinned butterfly, with the cypress piercing its centre and, all around it, the large ochre wings of the buildings' rooftops. Twenty craggy faces behind twenty cigarillos stare at me curiously. In their midst, a fully fledged member of the community, a donkey, lays down its curious head. The mayor comes forward, with outstretched hand and a snaggle-toothed smile.

The small crowd leads me, pushing and pulling, touching me to make sure that I really am the *professore*, the one from Paris, because they have never seen one here before and so, *scusi*, they don't know what one looks like. I am served a cup of coffee, the kind only Italians know how to make, a bitter, tar-like brew that reminds me of my childhood, when I would fall and graze my knee. First you don't feel anything, and then comes that sting that brings tears to your eyes . . . and the dizziness of relief when the pain fades.

I call them 'Italians' even though these people have been French since 1860. Three times since my arrival, the mayor has repeated 'real French people, *Professore*', a patriotic finger indicating his red, white and blue sash. But they have lost nothing of their native land, on the other side of the mountain peak. Everything about them speaks of stone. Their skin, their hands, the dust in their hair. It brings them into being and it kills them. Here, before becoming a bricklayer, a carpenter, a cuckold, before becoming a bandit, rich or poor, you are a mountaineer. It's hardly surprising. A child of these valleys meets a cliff face as soon as he can walk. He must learn to climb or he will go nowhere.

France? Italy? Doesn't matter. Those are merely the words of children, bickering as they push counters across a large map. We are nowhere, in the belly of the world, and this place belongs to nobody, only to the science that brings me here today. By evening, I am in the room booked in my name in the village's sole *locanda*. The air smells ancient. The discomfort is absolute. The shutters, pale purple and peeling, open onto a horizon in upheaval. A vertical landscape.

Beneath my window, a puppy flounders in the wall's shadow, whirling after its own tail. It does not yet know that it will never catch it, that others have tried before and given up the quest. I know that puppy. My lips open to call out its name. But no, of course, it is 16 July 1954 and Pépin has been dead for forty years.

I closed the door to my apartment a week ago; I say 'my' out of habit, but it was already no longer mine. I went to see Madame Mitzler on the sixth floor and told her I was leaving. *Where are you going?* Doesn't matter, Madame Mitzler, what matters is that I will no longer be there to help you carry your shopping upstairs on Fridays, to ask you to do my sewing for me, to rescue your cat when you leave the window open, to warn you when your sink overflows, enlarging the dark ring on my kitchen ceiling. *Will you come back?* Of course I'll come back, Madame Mitzler, what do you think? But probably not to this neighbourhood. I'll be in a more chic area, in an apartment with mouldings, perhaps. In her hazy eyes, I saw a mix of regret and admiration. Madame Mitzler knew a man of destiny when she saw one.

It was raining, a whine of grey zinc that trickled under collars. On the way to the Gare de Lyon, I passed the university that I had entered for the first time a quarter of a century before, a young palaeontology professor still full of illusions, certain that I had arrived in an Olympus where all pettiness would be banished. Only later did I learn that the gods of Olympus were pettier, crueller and more vicious than any human. The gods lied, plundered, cheated, devoured one another. But they were intelligent, no doubt about that.

The only thing I owe that place is Umberto. One day in my office, he appeared suddenly, giving me the fright of my life. How could this carnival giant have come in without me noticing? His clumsy movements, his awkward smile brought to mind a child perched on stilts under a papier mâché costume, using hidden levers to produce each comic gesture or expression. His thick-lensed glasses only added to this blundering impression. He had the seriousness of all giants, of all beings who occupy more space than ordinary mortals on this planet, and who bear the responsibility that goes with it: he had to measure the impact of his actions.

'I am your new assistant, Professor.'

Umberto was twenty years old, and I was twenty-five. Nobody had told me about his appointment; I had never had an assistant and I hadn't asked for one either. Nobody at the university knew what he was doing there. In the end, we found his name in a file in the accounts department, and that proved enough to justify his presence. If we were paying him, he must have some use – it stood to reason. It was only later that we realised he was part of an exchange programme between the universities of Paris and Turin. Despite an in-depth investigation, we were not able to work out the identity of the student we had misplaced in Turin.

Umberto rapidly became indispensable. I liked his calm presence, his devotion, the way he called me 'Professor', a title he respected all the more since I was so young. In this regard, he was the exact opposite of my colleagues, who, for the same reason, pronounced the word as if it were in quotation marks. He was not the most rigorous or intelligent scientist I knew. But there was magic in his hands. When an ammonite disintegrated in my fingers, when the stone refused to surrender the hostage that it held, it was Umberto I called. Gently, he released time's grip on the object that interested me: leaf, mollusc, fragment of bone. He acted with infinite slowness, a consequence, probably, of his childhood in the mountains. More than once, I found him in his office early in the morning, in exactly the same position as I had left him the previous evening: chisel in one hand, brush in the other, frozen in a dust cloud of atoms. He wasn't married, so it didn't really matter to him where he laid his large head to allow sleep to steal a few hours of his life.

After two years, I told him he could call me by my first name. A thousand times, I tried to make him pronounce *Stan,* explaining that the *n* was the final sound, but every time he said 'Stan-eh', his hands raised in a comic gesture of helplessness when he heard his own mistake. In the end I just laughed about it.

Then there was the story of the grappa. One evening, I went to the laboratory to look for a sample. Umberto was studying photographs of an excavation site in the Ardèche. Next to him stood an open bottle. The smell of alcohol assaulted my nostrils. Smiling, he offered me a swig; his uncle made very small amounts of this eau de vie and he had sent him a bottle to remind him of his home, where it was highly sought after. I said no. I didn't know how things worked in Turin. In France, and particularly in Paris, and more particularly in that venerable college, a researcher did not drink while working. Without a second thought, I confiscated the bottle from the sheepish giant and put it in a cupboard, where I promptly forgot about it.

I found it again by chance. It was late, and I had stayed behind to fill out a grant application. The bottle was half empty anyway, so who would notice? From the first mouthful, a mountain wind struck me, an aria of slopes and meadow flowers that brought tears to my eyes. I worked until midnight.

When I had finished with the form, I stood up to gather my belongings. Suddenly clumsy, I pitched forward head first into the field of edelweiss, dragging my chair and a few documents from my desk behind me. Alerted by the racket, Umberto came running. While he picked up the empty bottle, I gigglingly apologised. I was sorry – that divine drink had made me feel as if I were eating springtime, sorry, really sorry, Umberto, I never told you this before but you're my best friend, I swear it, my *meilleur ami,* come here and let me hug you, soon we'll have new grants and it's all thanks to your grappa, oh and you wouldn't have another bottle, would you, what was I saying, oh yeah, all granks to your thappa, why is that so hard to pronounce, um, but yeah, anyway, it's thanks to your grappa that I managed to finish that form.

'This form?'

He held the pink pages out in front of me. Only the first page had been correctly filled in. The rest was covered with sketches of dinosaurs, fossils, pretty landscapes. There was even a short poem. After that, I don't remember anything.

I woke in a disused storeroom in the building's bowels, huddled under a sheet of tarpaulin next to a puddle with my previous night's dinner floating in it. Bitterness on my tongue, my soul in shreds: I was twenty-seven years old and this was my first hangover. It would not be my last.

Umberto was asleep in my office, in the permanent twilight of all basements, his head resting on the grant application form, neatly filled out and ready to be sent. When I started apologising, he stretched out his arms, which were long enough to touch the walls, and interrupted me with a nonchalant *va bene*. Frustrated in my penitence (a legacy of the teachings of Abbé Lavernhe), I told him: 'All the same, if I were in your shoes, I'd be angry.'

'Back home, everybody tries to get our *zio* to tell them the secret of his grappa. You only needed one taste of it to understand. My uncle adds flowers to the grape marc before distilling it. You are a refined man with good tastebuds. So, no, I'm not angry.'

With those words, Umberto left me to my headache.

From then on, he always brought me some grappa whenever he received any . . . and I pretended not to notice when he drank it at his desk.

'Destination?'

It stopped raining the moment I arrived at the Gare de Lyon. I took that as a sign.

'Destination?' repeated the guy behind the counter.

'Nice,' I replied.

He handed me a ticket and said, 'Next.'

Four days. Still no Umberto. I've given up going to the bus stop to wait for him. I curse him, telling myself I'll wait one more day and then leave without him, even though I know perfectly well that this is not true. Everybody knows it: the birds, the stones, the cricket playing the violin on my thigh. I can't do anything without Umberto.

The village was almost deserted this morning, its inhabitants sucked into more prosperous, more open valleys, for a day or a week of labour. Some will not return. The most famous of those who left and never came back, the mayor told anyone who would listen, was his Capolungo cousin, the one who went to America, the one who succeeded in 'Ollyhoude'. Or that, at least, is what the cousin told everybody in the long letters he sent to the village. And what did it matter if it wasn't true? What did it matter if he was exaggerating when he spoke of boulevards so wide that you could get lost while you were crossing them, or of women who never got old? What did it matter if he was starving to death on a construction site somewhere, piling up rocks like all the men in the village? To leave was, in itself, to succeed.

I know America well. I miss it. Here, there is nothing but heat and a sprinkling of shade. This valley is a wound in the mountainside, an eternal vendetta between stone and water. It smells of church, the scent of the wind in the steeple, of tarnished bronze, of crosses lying in the grass. You expect silence, but your ears are wearied by a perpetual roar: the torrent rushing below, mint-sharp, where moss-covered steps sink into the water. You would have to be crazy to venture there.

I have not seen any children here. Either they are pacing the playgrounds of distant boarding schools or the people are born old. If I were from here, I too would want to stay as long as possible inside my mother's womb. I would only emerge when I had run out of space, in a crumpled suit, happy to have spared myself twenty or thirty years of vertigo under these steep grey mountainsides. And then I would leave, like the Capolungo cousin.

By 10 a.m., the heat is oppressive. A large plane tree breaks up the light. Alone in the mountain's closed fist, I lean against a fountain, my fingers in the water. Everything around me seems poor: the air, the earth, all of it. Pure illusion. A voice speaks to us across the centuries, whispering in the crevasses and in the weft of the wind. A treasure awaits . . . But there are so many tales of treasure. So nobody listens. Nobody believes. Nobody but me.

21 July 1954

The village's only telephone rings in the mayor's office. The mayor, who is feeding his chickens, runs in to answer it. He puts his sash back on to bring me the news in person. Someone is arriving on that day's shuttle bus.

Umberto, finally.

The bus deposits him with a hydraulic sigh before heading back towards a sea that, after a few nights here, I feel sure I have only imagined. My friend has not changed: the same corduroy suit with the same walking boots that made us laugh twenty years ago, the last time we saw each other. Nobody could look so much like a landscape – his native Dolomites. Umberto is a cliff face leaning over the world, a pile of geological strata that move with the slowness of a continent. A smile splits the vertical fractures of his face. His hand, enormous, envelops mine with surprising, almost submissive gentleness, even though he too now answers to the grand-sounding title of *Professore* in Turin.

When he moves and the valley reappears behind him, I notice that he is not alone. A smiling young man stands beside him. The bus slowly shrinks into the background, its rear windscreen a dazzle of sunlight, and the golden haze behind him gives the boy the dazed look of a character that has fallen from a fresco. Peter, announces Umberto: his young assistant at the University of Turin.

I do my best to hide my anger. Yes, anger is what I feel: one of those good old bristling rages that have forged my reputation. I did not explicitly ask Umberto to come alone, of course. I thought he had understood that this was important. A childish conspiracy, perhaps, but a conspiracy all the same, and you shouldn't bring your neighbours' son along just because he happens to be there and you think he might be bored, alone on his seesaw.

I turn to Peter, hand held out. 'Pleased to meet you.'

My first words to this kid are a lie.

Umberto has blue fingernails. Peter has blue fingernails. And so, of course, do I. We spent our childhoods on all fours on chalky plateaus, sifting through rocks on mountainsides, our fingers getting crushed when a mallet slipped. Our secret greeting, our sign of recognition, is to be found in those missing nails, bruised so many shades of blue – Prussian, cobalt, turquoise – from being soaked in the subterranean nights of a fossilised continent.

Sitting on a chair that trembles under his weight, in the mist of the fountain, Umberto pinches the handle of a coffee cup. Silent, he waits. I called him just a few weeks ago: could he give me two whole months? He asked only one question in return, the same question that everybody has been asking me recently: 'Destination?'

I told him about the cirque in the mountain. I recommended that he make all his arrangements as discreetly as possible. He did not ask why; he simply explained that he had to be back in mid-September for a routine operation. For all the rest, I could count on him. That was Umberto.

Beside him, Peter sizzles with impatience. Everything about him is narrow: torso, shoulders, face, his upper lip fringed with a little red moustache that you want to shave off against his will. Peter is German, on secondment from the University of Marburg. When he explains something (and he explains everything), his hands turn on his wrists like mad sunflowers.

'At fifteen, I entered a seminary, *ja?* At seventeen, I gave it up for science. I thought I was changing my life. And you know what I chose?'

Palaeoclimatology. *Palaiós*, ancient. Peter is a historian of fire and ice, of the sky's influence on the earth, beasts and men.

'In fact, nothing changed. I still spend all day long talking about fire and brimstone!'

Once you get him started, he won't shut up. But he is an excellent recruit, as I am beginning to realise.

'I am very honoured to be part of this expedition, Professor . . .'

'Stan.'

'Stan. I was just wondering . . . *Was suchen wir?* What are we looking for, exactly?'

I wanted to answer him, I swear I did. I even heard myself saying: very good question, young man, we are looking for . . .

A fly is trapped in the thick air of my bedroom. Sprawled on my bed, I watch it struggle. If it died, if it fell at just the right spot into a drop of resin, if that resin hardened, fossilised and became amber, hard and transparent, if that amber survived a few million years, somewhere safe where it wouldn't be damaged but not so safe that it would never be discovered, then that fly would, one day in the distant future, deliver to a researcher the secrets of our world. A simple fly that nobody cares about; a simple fly that contains the universe. The fauna, the flora, the sky of 1954, and you could casually smash it with your hand.

'*Tutto bene*, Stan-eh?'

Umberto's head pokes through the half-open door, floating above me like an anxious balloon.

'Yes, why?'

'You suddenly got up and left in the middle of a sentence. Peter is very worried.'

'Ah, yes.'

Perhaps my secret has become too heavy to be shared. Or perhaps it's fear, the fear that my prize will be taken from me, that someone other than me will be able to name him, another guy with blue fingernails and oversized ambitions.

'*Tutto bene, Berti*. Tell Peter I'm sorry. I needed to lie down. I'm just a little tired because of this heat.'

Umberto laughs like a pipe organ, the low vibrations transforming my small bedroom into a cathedral.

'We're not getting any younger. But it'll be like the good old days up there, won't it, Stan-eh?'

Yes, like the good old days. Minus our meagre wages, our eyesight ruined by dim lamps, the lectures that nobody listened to. And if I'm wrong, if my theory is proved false, this time it will not simply be a case of closing a file, of burying it in a cemetery of paperwork and starting over. My future depends on the success of this expedition. The chic neighbourhood, the mouldings, all of it, you understand? No, of course not, you can't possibly understand.

I just pat my former assistant on the shoulder. We will meet again at 8 p.m. in the lounge of the *locanda*, where the guide hired by Umberto should be waiting for us.

'Stan-eh, the kid's right . . . You're going to have to tell us what we're looking for.'

So here we are. No turning back now. Do you really want to know, Berti? I breathe in the air that sings like metal through the open window. If I had known the value of that heat, I never would have let it go.

'A dragon. We're looking for a dragon.'

'A dragon? What do you mean?'

I stared at the little girl who had just invited the creature into the conversation. I wasn't sure I'd heard her correctly.

The university bigwigs had chosen me to accompany them that evening, I didn't know why. I hated social events. I spent my days in the basement, in the drab glare of ceiling lights, a thousand leagues from the bronzed adventurer I had once imagined myself becoming. The existence suited me, the peaceful mole's life far from the great carnivores that prowled the surface. They had probably asked me along to inspire pity – you see, dear donors, how badly we need more money? – even if my worn elbows and my badly stitched hems owed more to Madame Mitzler's failing eyesight and trembling needle than to my university salary.

I arrived early outside the prestigious address. Chaos reigned in the building's courtyard – someone was moving out. I felt at ease in that disorder, and I lingered for no apparent reason among the piles of cardboard boxes. As a good scientist, I should have known that there was no such thing as chance. Behind each event were two hands rubbed together, a wandering star, a dog that leaves and does not return, billions of cogs spinning for aeons. Ever since – *bang* – nothing became something.

A little to the right or a little to the left, a second earlier or a second later, and I would have missed it. A fragment of bone. There, on the corner of a crate, ready to fall back inside at the faintest breath of air, to return to the oblivion from which it had come. Solid, broken along lines that complicated its identification, at least without more sophisticated analysis tools. A piece of tail or vertebra. Shiny brown, absence of porosity, advanced fossilisation. Cretaceous or Jurassic. Triassic? Unlikely.

I jumped when a removal man approached to close the crate's lid. The concierge was dead, an old man found after three days in his lodge, his body stiff. He had no family and his belongings were now the property of the State. The man took the bone from my hands, put it back in the crate, and stood there watching me suspiciously, waiting for me to leave before he got back to work.

Our hosts told me nothing more during dinner. The concierge had been there for ever, an old Italian who never spoke to anybody and who, in recent years, had not been entirely sane. He was lazy, grouchy. 'He smelled,' said the mistress of the house. 'He used to hit the bottle very early,' her husband added. They couldn't fire him because he received a disability allowance. The only thing they didn't reproach him for was being dead.

I would not be in this little room in the back of beyond, five years later, balanced precariously on the edge of the world, had I not wandered through the apartment that evening in search of the bathroom. But wander I did. A little girl appeared in an explosion of freckles and tugged at my sleeve.

'Are you a friend of Monsieur Leucio's?'

In response to my frown, she added: 'I heard you talking about him with Papa.'

The old concierge? I shook my head.

'He was nice. He had a dragon.'

'A dragon? What do you mean?'

She whispered so that her parents wouldn't hear. When the adults were away, the old concierge would gather the building's children in a circle, under a single bare bulb in the cellar, and tell them stories. The most popular story among this juvenile secret society was the one about his dragon. *Ora, ascoltatemi bene ragazzi*, now listen closely,

27

children . . . As a teenager, Leucio had got lost after sneaking away from home to go and see a girl. For three days, he had wandered. A huge storm erupted and he ran beneath an electric sky to take refuge in a cave. There, he found himself face to face with *un drago di tuono e di lampo*, a dragon of thunder and lightning.

The old man was speaking: I could hear his gravelly voice behind the little girl's high-pitched squeak. He talked about an immense skeleton, a body sunk in darkness, stretching out so far that he could not see where it ended, a surprisingly small head at the end of an enormous neck. The dragon had protected the young man from the storm. It had spoken to him.

A familiar pain roared through my veins, an old pain that I knew well. It was life stirring within me, as it had that time when I'd had the idea of walking across the frozen lake so I could get to school more quickly, and had fallen through the ice into the water. It took them a quarter of an hour to resuscitate me; the doctor even told me afterwards that, technically speaking, I had been dead for a few minutes. All I remember is a big crack, and then the blood roaring through my white veins. That is the pain I am talking about.

Where did he come from, little one, that concierge? Did he mention the name of the valley where he lived? But the girl knew nothing. I asked for other details – what cave? How could I recognise it? The kid's face lit up beneath the red freckles. The cave was at the base of a glacier, she recited in her chiming voice. From there, you could see three mountain peaks shaped like pyramids and crowned with lightning. That was all she could recall, her short memory saturated with tragedies and wonders.

Over the next few days, I managed to find out the concierge's full name. He had barely left a mark on the world that he had exited one spring evening, in a lodge that stank of sewage. He had no family. But every man leaves behind him a sticky trail, a series of administrative traces, which I followed with the obsessive patience of someone whose profession forces him to think in terms of millions of years.

I wrote to the registry office, the town hall, the immigration office, asking where this old man had come from, attempting to discover the valley where his dragon was sleeping. I didn't get any further than Melun. The concierge's official existence began there, in a military hospital, on a yellowed form. Twenty years old and a heart murmur: *Exempted*. What had come before this, nobody knew.

Years passed. My letters went missing, dried out on shelves, or returned to me intact, stained with foreign dust. My phone calls rang in empty offices. In the end I gave up, convincing myself that it was nothing more than a story for adventure-deprived Parisian children invented by a homesick old man. I focused on my work; I applied for a grant that I felt sure I would get, and that would involve me spending a few months at the Natural History Museum in London. Case closed.

And then, six months ago, a parcel arrived, accompanied by a letter of apology. The postmark was edged with transalpine flourishes, ink lions whose phoney roars frightened nobody. The letter came from an Italian government office, signed by an obscure bureaucrat who assured me of his highest consideration. It mentioned a lost stack of folders, a fire that had destroyed some official documents. Except this one, enclosed in the envelope: Leucio D.'s birth certificate, with the name of his village. And his marriage certificate in the same valley, eighteen years later. Well, almost the same valley: the annexation of the County of Nice, in 1860, had made it French.

I ran from the university to the Rue des Écoles to buy a map. There, I found the three mountain peaks, backing onto Italy. Sentinels watching over the glacier, folds of pink lines on a grey background, between Mercantour and Argentera. To someone who could read maps, those contour lines evoked a hostile, terrifying verticality. One false step to the right, you would die Piedmontese. To the left, you would die French. The dragon was well protected, at the centre of a stone cirque that men of old must have believed inhabited by the gods.

There were no gods, up there or anywhere else. But an expedition would have only two months, three at the most, to work at that altitude. As soon as the first snow fell, the place would be cut off from the rest of the world and would return to nothingness. I caressed the map, imagining the beast beneath my fingertips, asleep in his paper cave.

Less than an hour later, my telephone rang. Despite the renowned quality of my work, the grant had been given to someone else; it was a delicate matter, rather political in fact – you understand, don't you, Stan? The university vice chancellor promised me his personal support. I was sure to receive the grant the next time it was awarded. As sure as one could be of anything in such a profession, anyway. In other words, not very.

The yellow walls of my tiny apartment fell apart like a rickety movie set.

'Hello? Stan?'

A meadow stretched out as far as I could see all around me, rising gently towards misty foothills. I was sitting on a chair behind a ridiculous desk. I had become reasonable without even realising it.

'Stan, are you still there?'

I stood up and disappeared into the mist.

While we wait for our guide, I explain everything to Umberto and Peter. At last they know why they are here: to make history, to hunt it down instead of waiting like scavengers for whatever remnants are thrown their way.

'An apatosaurus?' suggests Peter. 'A diplodocus? Or . . .'

His eyes light up. I guess what he is going to say, because we have the same fingernails.

'Or a *brontosaurus*.'

The same fingernails, and the same dreams.

'Or a unicorn,' Umberto said tersely.

Umberto was banned from Sunday school at a very young age, he once told me, for asking what God's shoe size was. A scientist does not unquestioningly swallow a tall tale without demanding some proof, some concrete detail. Doubt is our religion.

'Imagine a kid of thirteen or fourteen, Berti. Imagine him alone in a storm, frightened, exhausted. He finds a perfectly preserved dinosaur skeleton. He is completely uneducated. The creature is huge. It looks like nothing he has ever seen.'

'Why keep it secret if it's true?'

'Because the dragon spoke to him. Because he had a fever, hallucinations. Because he was superstitious. I don't know why! Who cares why?'

Umberto grimaces. His fingers knead his cheeks and work his jaw as if to punish it for what he is about to say.

'Or he just invented it. A story for some bored Parisian kids.'

'Except that . . .'

Follow the dots. There's one detail that has escaped everybody.

'Except that, if it was a story for children,' Umberto murmurs, 'why not describe the head as enormous, frightening, with huge sharp teeth? Why would a simple countryman describe the head as being too small for the rest of the body, anatomically correct for a diplodocid?'

I slam my palm down on the table, so hard that the other two jump. 'Exactly!'

'There have been no major fossil discoveries in the region,' the giant objects.

'A stupid, unscientific argument.'

For an instant I fear I have upset him, that I have counter-attacked too hard in my excitement, but Umberto accepts defeat with good grace. Peter leans unthinkingly towards whoever is speaking before seeking out the other's response in a pendulum movement that would have made me laugh were it not for the irritating creaking noise that his chair makes each time he does this.

'Listen to me, Umberto. All your objections, I've already made them. All of them. After that, I invented others. But remember the fragment of bone I saw in Leucio's belongings . . . His description of the glacier, its position between the three mountain peaks . . . it all fits. Am I certain? Nobody could be. So, imagine: maybe a brontosaurus, as Peter said, the chance to prove that Marsh was right and that it is a distinct species from the apatosaurus. Even if it's an apatosaurus or a diplodocus, we're talking about a *complete* skeleton. Not a puzzle that we'll have to painstakingly restore using guesswork and plaster. It would be the Holy Grail for any museum director or university vice chancellor. We are maybe a few days' journey from one of the most incredible creatures to have ever walked the earth. A giant that will engrave our names in history.'

'*Your* name, Stan-eh.'

He's right: that's the tradition. Ladies and gentlemen, Stan the dinosaur, *Titanosaurus stanislasi*, the pièce de résistance of London's Natural History Museum. Scissors, ribbon, the curtain falls, gasps and wide eyes as the largest fossil discovery of the last one hundred years is unveiled.

'And the university is funding all this?' my friend asks.

'Luckily. Although you know them – it wasn't easy. I had to do some arm-twisting.'

'So what's your plan?'

'Three scenarios. One, we discover the cave and the skeleton quickly – let's say in two weeks. We separate the head and bring it back with us. That would be ideal, the dream scenario. Two, we take longer than expected to find it and don't have time to take a sample before we return. We photograph it, we measure it, and we come back next year. The discovery will be ours and we'll have proof. Three . . .'

Everybody knows the third possibility. I screwed up. I swallowed the babblings of a crazy old man out of laziness or, worse, out of weakness. Because when I listen to Alfred Deller sing *Vergnügte Ruh* on Madame Mitzler's record player while she hems my trousers, there's a lump in my throat. Because I'm going soft.

Peter raises his glass of grappa, eyes shining.

'If we're not capable of believing a story just because it's a good one, what is the point of this job?'

Thanks, kid. Umberto in turn raises his glass and smiles fawningly.

'To Stan-eh, the dinosaur.'

Vergnügte Ruh. Joyful peace. It doesn't take much.

Our guide arrived at the end of a baking hot night. The man entered amid caramel heat, greeted by grunts and averted eyes, which, in this world where nothing is like the rest of the world, are signs of respect.

Gio is an old Italian, the favourite guide for English mountaineers who come here to steal the height that is lacking in their own country. The mountains change, but he is always the one they call, the world over. Or rather they call his neighbour, the one with the telephone, who runs to fetch Gio from some roof in the village. And Gio puts down his roofer's tools, picks up his bag and his leather shoes, says goodbye to his wife, swears that this will be the last time – he's lying, and they both know it – and he leaves. Switzerland, France, Italy, the Himalayas. Gio is expensive: I almost choked when Umberto told me the price. Gio is expensive because he's not dead. He has climbed Annapurna, the Eiger, the Matterhorn and other mountains, and he is not dead. He has never slipped or fallen, either because he is lucky or because he is the best. Both come at a price.

Our guide is thin and wiry; he is neither pleasant nor unpleasant. Wherever he is, you have the impression that he has always been there. No past, no future, just there. Umberto and he are from the same village, about three hundred miles from here; that is how they know each other. Gio is ten years older than Umberto. He speaks a Venetian dialect that Umberto translates in an undertone, a rare patois full of solitary consonants and strange repetitions that sound like gunfire.

Gio could not care less about the aim of our expedition. Climb up, survive, climb down – that is his Holy Trinity. He spreads out a map and places a bony finger upon it. There it is, the path that I spotted, the only one that allows access to the stone cirque. *Allowed* – past tense. It was swept several hundred metres away by an avalanche two winters ago. As for what remains of it, Gio does not want to go there.

But. His finger moves.

There is another way, known to only a handful of men: a via ferrata created long ago by smugglers. Elevated, dangerous in places. Are we capable of negotiating it? Umberto is a born mountaineer – *sì*. Peter, too, has done some climbing in his youth – *ja*. But I am not fit or athletic. Worse, I suffer from vertigo.

'Stan-eh?'

'No problem.'

Gio lays down the rules. Up there, in our stone fortress one and a half miles above sea level, we will obey his every command. We must take as few metal objects as possible. The mountain is so rich in iron that lightning is always drawn to it. If the mission takes longer than expected, he will decide when it is time to come back down, just before the bad weather begins. '*Aeo intendù?*'

Umberto cracks his knuckles.

''*Son a ciatà fora chel mostro!* Let's hunt the monster!'

And Gio mutters: '*Là su, i mostre l é solo chi che te te portes drio.*'

This time, I don't need a translation to understand the law of the mountain.

Up there, the only monsters are the ones you take with you.

Night is still sticking to the mountains, a thick, inky paste that will be hard to lift. Gio had been waiting for us when we emerged from the *locanda* a little earlier, staggering under the weight of our brand-new rucksacks. Sitting on the edge of a drinking trough, he was smoking one of those twisted Toscanos that scorch your throat. I've seen grown men cry at their first puff and thirteen-year-old kids sucking them like liquorice. The cigar's smell, in the languor of dawn, was reminiscent of the air after a lightning strike.

A convoy was waiting, swallowed up by the darkness. Three donkeys with worn coats like velvet, leaning on one another so as not to collapse. Each carried a red metal container on one side, a pack on the other. A farmer, wedged against them, was sleeping on his feet. *That* was my expedition? I had sent a large sum of money to Umberto the previous month, for these three old nags? Four, if you counted the old man . . .

By gesturing towards the mountain peaks, invisible in the blackness, then towards his ludicrous donkeys, I communicated to Gio: them, not enough, me, not happy. Not happy at all. I was not about to be swindled by a bunch of country bumpkins. And I knew country bumpkins, because I was one. I, too, knew how to rig a scale on market days by weighing down the tray or removing a couple of fruit just before packaging them. My father had showed me. Gio exhaled a huge puff of cigar smoke before sucking it back in through his nostrils: it would have been stupid to waste good second-hand smoke in this land where everything is so rare. He spoke too fast for me to understand.

'Tell him those lousy donkeys are not enough, Berti. I'm no sucker.'

'They're just here to transport the oil for the lamps and the fire. Everything else is already up there.'

'Everything else?'

'Most of the oil, the tents, the firewood, some provisions of dried meat, the tools and stuff that we'll need to catch a few rabbits to brighten up our everyday fare. Gio's men took everything up last week.'

'They . . . On the via ferrata?'

Gio shrugged and muttered a response that was instantly translated by Umberto.

'About nine hundred pounds of equipment.'

With the dab of a paintbrush, dawn reddens the sky and outlines the cliffs.

'And they're actually mules, not donkeys.'

If anyone ever takes an interest in my life, I will pass over this episode in silence. The stuff about rigging scales as well.

The mountain path has petered out. There is now no more than a trickle of stones beneath our feet, occasionally punctuated by an orgy of roots. The valley is narrowing and sheering. We can hardly hear the river any more. Above our heads, the spruces are racing the granite cliffs towards the sky. Arrogance in defeat: therein lies the nobility of those trees. The heat has returned, even more intense than before, filling the narrow pass with an incandescent haze.

I have never felt at ease in the mountains. As a child, I saw them from below. They were called the Pyrénées, but at six I heard this as *Pires Aînés*. The worst elders. I imagined older brothers, immense and terrifying, of another race, probably evil. Maybe that was why we didn't climb them. As soon as you set foot on a mountain, the question is direct, almost stark. 'Are you sure about this? You didn't make a mistake?' The mountain has questioned me a thousand times this morning and I haven't known how to reply. Sometimes I have the feeling I am getting close, that the next curve is hiding a secret, a variation. But the trees all look the same and the stone remains. Umberto and Gio walk ahead, one behind the other, left right left right, ambling like camels. Behind, Peter patiently waits for me to move forward. He doesn't pass me when I stop, a mark of deference that gives me the impression that I am slowing everybody down. Last come our three donkeys – sorry, mules – and the villager whose name I don't know. He'll take the animals back when they can no longer continue.

At noon, we take a lunch break. A rectangle of dried meat, some hard bread rubbed with garlic, and a few mouthfuls of metallic-tasting water. Then we fold away our knives, put our rucksacks on our backs, and recommence our interminable attack, human atoms eroding the mountain like the water, wind and ice before us.

A miracle has occurred. I have found my mountain legs. They were there, by the side of the path, waiting for me, and I put them on without even realising. They are wonderful legs, full of contained power, spring and technique for coping with the treacheries of the path. Suddenly I am light on my feet, and soon I walk close behind Umberto, who gives me a knowing little smile. I am one of them now.

Lying on my sleeping bag under a streak of stars. The first day of an expedition that might last ten or a hundred, it's impossible to say. There's a rock digging into my shoulder. But I can't move, my body is too weary. My new legs have been neatly put away just below my waist – I wouldn't want to wear them out too quickly. Behind the horizon, a dragon stretches out its immense neck and roars into the night. *I'm waiting for you.* My eyes close amid a scent of everlasting flowers, a fragrance of brides and old women, of eternal renewal.

Soon.

The Commander was my father. Everybody called him that, in the bar, on the street, at the market, even though he was a farmer without any military glory in his past. It was said that the name came from a beating he had once given to a guy from the next village, who had looked at him the wrong way. Leaning over the man as he lay in a pool of his own blood, my father had yelled: 'So, who's in command, eh? Who's in command?' The name stuck.

One day, a Spanish seasonal worker came into our living room, his face grave with dust and sweat.

'*Un pépin à la grange, jefe.*'

Something went wrong in the barn, boss.

About fifty crates of apples had been knocked over, their contents scattered. The guilty party was lying in the middle of this disorder: a blue merle puppy with one ear folded over, asleep, with a fruity bubble at the corner of its mouth. Pépin – the something that went wrong – entered my life without any explanation, just as he would later leave it.

He followed me everywhere. His youth and mine mingled in a whirlwind that left us panting, tongues lolling, knees grazed. Soon he grew stronger, faster, more cunning than me, and I raged at being trapped in a body that was too small. Pépin's world was round and I was its centre. He encircled me in an attentive dance, drifting further and further away, so that by the time I was nine and he was four, I guessed at his presence more than I saw it. But he was still there, flashing on the edges of my life like a speck of dust on an eyelash.

*

At school, I was a loner. I preferred reading to sports and hunting, which was enough to classify me unambiguously as a pansy. To prove that his son was no sissy, and to boost my popularity, the Commander organised a birthday party to which he invited my schoolmates. It didn't matter to him that it wasn't my – or any of my friends' – birthday. He shoved us into the barn with a leather ball: have fun, kids. After a few limp passes, they made me the goalkeeper. The goal was a narrow space between two haystacks. The others quickly realised that it was more fun to aim at me than to score a goal. I somehow managed to dodge all their shots until Castaings, the mayor's son, knocked me off my feet, as stars danced before my eyes and distorted laughter rang in my ears. They sat me up and wedged me against the wall. One of the Etcheberry twins got ready to take a penalty kick.

Castaings raised his hand to give the signal. Then suddenly vanished, snatched away in a growl of shadow by the darkness behind him. After a second of stunned silence, the others ran off screaming. When I opened my eyes, I was alone in the barn, with Pépin sitting in front of me. My dear old Pépin. I hadn't seen him this close in weeks. My fingers sank into his coat below his ears, where it was thickest, and I buried my face there to breathe in his smell of warm cake, candied fruit and sun-baked honey. He was much bigger than he had been in my memory.

Castaings escaped with eleven stitches, the others with the fright of their lives. The Commander made a generous donation for the refurbishment of the church. In return, Abbé Lavernhe helped the mayor to obtain the annulment of his first marriage. The mayor decided not to press charges.

In the village, the rumour spread that I could talk to animals. Among the more simple-minded, it was said that I had dealings with the devil. My popularity never recovered. I came to understand that it was better to seek friends in the depths of rock and clay, and – if you didn't find any there – to invent them.

We hear it – a soft song of wool, a melody of hooves. We smell it – a breath of wet slate. But we don't see it: the border is invisible. The border of a nation as vast as the wind, whose few inhabitants speak the language of animals. At noon we enter the land of the shepherds.

At the narrowest part of the pass, a log bridge spans the river. The horizon opens up and unfurls over a vast plateau. The heat is still there, dry and white like the edge of a knife. Sharper and just as painful. The plateau seems to end in a cul-de-sac. No cirque, no mountain peak solidifies the horizon.

'Shouldn't we be able to see the three peaks now? Leucio's landmarks? Are you sure we're on the right path?'

Gio: '*Na croda, no te pos saé se te ra ciataras ancora agnoche te r as lasciada.*'

Umberto: 'With a mountain, you never know if you'll find it where you left it.'

The two men continue to advance with the same serious expressions. I have just sampled the sibylline wisdom of the Dolomites. Either that or these rough creatures have a sense of humour that I had never suspected before.

The grass in this country is traversed by clear water, little fledgling rivers that leave their nests for the first time and wander out into the great world. Cracks appear in the slab of heat, veins of coolness that we come upon unexpectedly. They slap us in the face, stop us in our tracks. We want to follow them back to their source, but we must continue straight towards the fleeing horizon.

'What the . . .!'

Peter bursts out laughing like a child – my foot has disappeared into a hole filled with water. Then he freezes like an attentive dog, finger pointed towards a vein of gneiss. Since our departure, he has swung between moods as nimbly as an acrobat. Now he remarks, very seriously – because he would never joke about such things – on the phenomenon of tectonic uplift that first formed this tortured region nearly forty million years before.

Forty million years. These figures no longer amaze me as they did once, when I was trying to construct a timescale on the floor of my bedroom, one matchstick for every thousand years, and I realised with terror that my outstretched arms could not reach from the present to the birth of the mountains. For that, I would have needed arms stretching all the way out to the barn. They'd have had to go far beyond that, to the peach orchard, to reach a diplodocus. And I couldn't go to the peach orchard anyway, since I'd have had to pass through the living room, where my parents were yelling. So I pushed my matchsticks closer together and moved the furniture out of the way, allowing me to stay inside my room.

Forty million years wasn't old. Leucio's dragon lived a hundred million years *before* the plateau's formation. I had become used to such grandeur. You can become used to anything: to the collision of planets, to the shifting of continents, to trilobites so distant on my timescale that I would no longer be on my father's property but in Abbé Lavernhe's garden.

Nothing surprises me any more. Perhaps that is why I sometimes feel sad. Or is it because, as my mother used to say, our family has sadness in its veins?

Tonight we camp on the edge of the plateau. At this point, it narrows suddenly and veers eastwards, looking from a distance like a dead end. At the far end of this black gorge, the final ascent awaits us.

Night has fallen, the air feels lighter. Unthinkingly, Umberto hums an old folk tune. Dots of fire sparkle behind us on the slopes: the campfires of the shepherds whom we saw during the day from a distance. Tall, mute figures, they responded to our friendly waves with a gesture that looked like a benediction.

I could easily fall asleep like this, with my chin on my knees, but it's impossible because Peter won't stop talking. With the zeal of a preacher, he details the rock formations that surround us.

'Typically anatexic . . . *hervorragend* example of migmatites . . . and that rift over there . . .'

A lunar howl rings out and spreads across the horizon. Another joins it, then another, forming a warrior chorus that my primate genes have not forgotten. No words, but the message is clear: *Run, you idiot.*

'Did you hear that?'

'*Ja. Wölfe.*'

'There are wolves here?'

'*Ja.* Either that or really big marmots.'

The others guffaw. Not me.

'There are wolves here and you think it's funny?'

Umberto's voice overlaps Gio's reassuring Venetian drone.

'The shepherds aren't afraid of them. Just one of their dogs can stand up to several wolves. Attacks are rare.'

'And up there? We won't have any dogs with us.'

I have history when it comes to wolves. As a little kid, I would hear them running in silent hordes down the slopes to the north of the farm, their eyes flashing inside my cupboard, under my chest of drawers; they would slip between the cracks, wherever the night existed, and our house was full of both: cracks and the night. And I couldn't escape to the safety of my mama's bed because the Commander had decreed that, at six years old, such solace was forbidden. Sleeping in your mama's bed was enough to make a boy a pansy. Or, worse, a queer.

Gio starts laughing. *Loe no in é, agnoche son drio a 'sì.* There are no wolves where we're headed, he explains, unless they've grown hands so they can climb a via ferrata. Or unless they've found a path that we don't know about. The old guide leans down, picks up a piece of schist, and holds it up to me.

'You want to be afraid of something? Be afraid of this. It'll smash your skull. It'll break loose in your hands. It'll split you in two, it'll bury you, it'll skin you alive. Here, stone is more dangerous than any wolf.'

W*alk without thinking.*
We have left colour behind. Everything is grey, even the green of the lichen. The path, bordered by slopes running with stones, climbs from the bottom of an immense furrow. If the mountain wanted to lure us into a trap, this is exactly how it would go about it.

Or think about something other than tiredness.

The rock sings, it chimes like crystal at each footstep. Sometimes it slips away like liquid beneath your feet, and the next thing you know you are on your knees, your hand cut open by a sharp ridge.

In 1879, Charles Marsh discovers a species that he names brontosaurus.

A shape emerges from the nothingness, a grey presence on the horizon. Suddenly there it is. A rocky face where winds and birds crash, a roar of stone thrusting towards the sky, three hundred metres above.

Marsh's colleagues – I know them well because they are just like mine – emphasise that the fossil's missing head makes it impossible to identify it officially. They declare that the skeleton is merely the adult version of a young apatosaurus discovered by Marsh himself two years earlier, not a new species. They shake hands and come to an agreement: the brontosaurus does not exist.

The villager releases the mules, which almost immediately set off in the opposite direction.

The brontosaurus does not exist . . . until someone proves that it does. Any palaeontologist would sell his parents to find one. In any case, I

45

would sell my father, without hesitation. But to find one, I must . . .

Climb the via ferrata: sharp metal bars like staples in the granite, horizontal rods marking a lateral path still visible from where we stand. Thousands of pairs of feet have shaped this path before ours, this vertiginous passage where salt, tobacco, oil have been carried by men, hired dirt-cheap for the season by the salt makers of Aigues-Mortes.

You are going to die here. This is no place for the weak. You are going to die in the void with your smuggler's dreams. And if the void doesn't kill you, the wolves will.

Peter, Umberto and Gio are harnessed. The guide checks the equipment of the other two before taking care of me. He works without looking at me. The rope spurts like a snake between his fingers, encircling my waist, my groin, my waist again.

Tell them to go to hell. You can't climb that.

'You okay, Stan-*eh*? You're white as a sheet.'

'Just a bit out of breath.'

'We're leaving the oil cans here. Gio will come back to get them while we're working.'

'*Welch eine unglaubliche Landschaft!* What an incredible landscape! I can't wait for Yuri to see this.'

Scent of oxide. The first steps of the via ferrata are cold as ice and I do not yet know that there will be a fifth member of our expedition.

The Valley of Hell. The Devil's Horn. This region is full of infernal names and I am beginning to understand why. With each step, with each bar that I climb, breathing in rust, my body doubles in weight. Fear steels my neck and shoulders.

An interminable wrench from the grips of gravity. This ascent is not so different from my childhood, in fact. When I told my parents that I wanted to become a palaeontologist, the Commander gave me a slap that made my ears ring until evening and told me to stop putting on airs. I would take over the family business, and that was the end of it. I confessed my scientific ambitions to Abbé Lavernhe, but God's representative in our parish was more concerned with training the local soccer team than with science. Any answers a man might need were to be found in the Bible or in the sports section of *La Dépêche*, and it was pointless to '*m'espoumper la cape de mul de craques pour bestiou*' – to cram my head full of twaddle for morons.

One day, I wanted to know why the Commander didn't like fossils. My mother explained, in a serious voice, that you had to be beautiful to see them, to really see them. She gave me distant errands to run, errands that allowed me to search the surrounding fields. I hid my findings in the linen closet and we would admire them together by moonlight. It's true that she was beautiful.

Another step, and another. Letting go of the main ladder to grab a handrail and follow a ledge no wider than your foot. The worst moment, the one that makes my vision flash red, the one that I must suffer through again and again, is when I unfasten the snap hook that connects me to life so I can attach it to another rope or another bar. In that instant, vertigo engulfs me, it slips between my body and the rock wall and tries to push me into the void. Below me, Peter sings as he climbs. Whatever you do, don't close your eyes. One long blink and it'll all be over.

Here we go, another step.

Stuck. So close to the top that it's laughable. Only one more ladder, ten metres, and I'm at the summit. But if I lift a single finger, I will die. For an hour, Umberto and Peter have taken turns coming back down to encourage me, excoriate me, reason with me: I can't fall. Even if I did fall, the snap hook would hold me in place. A rope doesn't break – or 'very rarely', Peter specifies with a scientific rigour that makes me want to kill him. Gio smokes on the crest, legs dangling in the void. Say what you like, but I'm not the craziest man on this expedition.

Ten metres above me, the three men confer. Gio comes down,

bouncing around at the end of a rope, the remains of his cigar between his teeth. He stops next to me, inhales a puff of smoke, then abandons it to the wind. For once, I can understand his mutterings without Umberto's help.

'Take your time. But we're going on.'

He disappears upwards as quickly as he came down, sucked into the sky. I am alone.

I know Gio well enough by now to understand that he is sincere. He is ready to leave me here, to come and get me later, after I've fallen asleep or fainted, hanging at the end of my rope like a suicidal spider. This man, like all mountaineers, is insane, I am sure of it. I start climbing.

Twenty-fourth of July. Below me is the place I have spent months imagining. It is an elongated plateau, the courtyard of a fortress whose walls we have just scaled. The interior slopes are steep but negotiable, the bottom covered with short and dazzlingly green grass. The shape of the cirque, Peter theorises, must attract storms and encourage rain. I use words like 'cirque', 'courtyard' and 'plateau' because I am constructing a legend and these words seem more evocative to me than 'a combe in an anticlinal fold', the technical name for this particular geological formation.

If my instincts are correct, if Leucio wasn't a big fat liar, all it will take is a phone call to an English colleague to set the machine in motion. The scientific articles, the admiration, the society events that I will no longer despise. Farewell to the yellow office in the obscurity of a French university. Farewell to the trousers with the left leg longer than the right, to the people looking through me, turning away from me. I will take Madame Mitzler to see Deller at the opera house, then we will go to a chic restaurant, the Tour d'Argent perhaps, and when I ask if they are still serving, because it will be late by then, they will say: of course, monsieur, for a customer like you. I will burn candles for my mother, all night, all day, in every church in the world, until the world runs out of wax.

The setting sun glints off the glacier that encloses the opposite side of the combe, our ultimate objective. Gio has already started descending the succession of sloping ledges. Peter follows him. Umberto gives me a jowly nod and goes after them. I stand still, deeply moved. I have just seen an eagle fly past . . .

. . . and I had to look *down* to watch it.

Gio serves us some plum eau de vie to reward us for our efforts. My hand trembles as I hold the metal flask. It's the aftershock. My mind has finally understood the scale of what my body just did and it is making me pay.

There is nothing we can do now, except to wait. Around us, the combe is a solid block of obsidian. The silence is absolute; it fills our mouths, sticks to our teeth. We are the sole trace of life in a world of prayer. Even our fire burns silently, out of respect.

The main tent, the one with our food supplies stored inside, has been erected in a spot sheltered from rockslides in summer and from avalanches in winter; it is far from those countless edges, invisible to the untrained eye, along which lightning likes to run its burning fingers. We have enough provisions to last us an eternity – mostly meat and dried fruit. Every three days, a villager will leave some fresh produce, which Gio will descend the via ferrata to collect. Our equipment – ice axes, mallets, burins, and other metal objects – is stored in another area, under large oiled tarps. Each of us has his own tent, and they are shaped like nothing I have ever seen before. The hoops, made from hazel wood by Gio, are curved. The wind cannot get a grip on them, he explained to us. *Ma canche tira vento, tegnìve dura ra vostra anema.* But when the wind blows, hold on to your soul.

The glacier is an hour's walk. If our dragon wanted to play hide-and-seek with us, I wouldn't mind at all. After counting for so long, one arm over my eyes, it would be anticlimactic to find it right away, its tail poking out of a cupboard.

My hand is less shaky now. The fire has fallen asleep, lulled by its own crackling. Gio kicks it back into life, feeds it with a half-log. The flames jump – okay, okay, we're awake – and dance the tarantella from one piece of wood to the other. Umberto's hand goes to his pocket, hesitates, then finally takes out a photograph which is passed around the fire until it reaches me. A black-and-white picture of a young girl with slightly heavy features and bright eyes, a rustic beauty.

'My fiancée.'

I'm stunned. The world teeters on its axis.

'Your fiancée.'

'*Sì*. I'm getting married this winter.'

'You're in love?'

'*Sì*.'

'*You?* Umberto? The guy who wanted to know God's shoe size?'

'Laura told me God's shoe size.'

Laura works with Umberto at the University of Turin. I never imagined that he would get married one day, although it is hard for me to explain why. The long hours spent in the laboratory? Many of our colleagues work similar hours and have a perfectly normal family life: wife, children, mistress. I was married myself once, an ill-fated collision of existences that is not worth mentioning. But Umberto? Umberto is a mountain. It's as if Mount Everest fell in love with Audrey Hepburn.

Peter starts singing a guttural hymn. Gio reacts with the most joyful expression I have ever seen on his face: a slight crease around the eyes and a twitch of the lips, as if his mouth wanted to smile but didn't know how. He pours us some more eau de vie.

Umberto, in love.

Well, why not? Who says mountains don't have feelings? The sunrise makes them blush, after all.

A glacier, close up.

It's something that everyone should see at least once in their life: the Earth sticking out an enormous, cracked tongue, licking itself in curiosity, catching if it can any mountaineers who dare to venture there. How many lives have ended there, in a giant blue crunch, in the hard silence of this fishless sea?

The moraine gives way beneath our feet, two steps forward, one step back. We're out of breath when we reach the ice. We sit down and put on crampons – it's impossible to go on without them.

'There!'

We saw it at the same time as Peter: the black opening in the wall, about three hundred metres away. I start to move, but Gio holds me back. With his foot he tests the snow spread out before us, soft and white as a quilt, and it collapses with a sigh. Below, the glacier opens its greedy mouth, shading from azure to aquamarine, and it's so beautiful that I almost want to throw myself in anyway. Gio saved my life.

Roped together now, using ice axes, we advance. Cheeks burning, the skin on our fingers cracking like an old glove, each step is exhausting. This is real snow, not the friendly powder that Pépin and I used to love disturbing; this is the snow of glaciation, of eternal winters. One hour later, the cave hasn't moved – it looks the same distance from us as it did before. My three companions move like the mules that accompanied us from the village, their heads nodding slowly as they advance.

Suddenly I hear it. Beneath our crampons, the glacier is singing. My comrades, with their educated ears, hear its music, follow its tempo. I am clumsier, treading on the planet's toes. Little by little, my footsteps start to match theirs. My technique becomes smoother, my breathing more regular. I no longer look at the horizon, but down at my feet. They size up the mountain.

I admire Umberto even more than the others. Gio is short and wiry, and Peter is a young whippersnapper, so it's no surprise to see those two progressing so easily. Umberto, though, is six foot five, a universe in himself, a watchtower that refuses to remain in position. And yet he has a grace that transcends all logic. His feet barely sink into the snow. The altitude must have gone to my head. Either that or Umberto has feet like snowshoes. No, there's something else about him: I have the impression that he moves in several dimensions at the same time, dividing his weight between them. He barely makes a mark on our world.

Three hours after leaving the camp, we finally arrive at the cave. The opening is higher than I thought, a good ten metres above the ice. Gio takes more ropes and pitons from his bag.

Titanosaurus stanislasi. You're not going to spare me anything, are you?

Four men huddle around a fire. The vast night sticks to their backs and pushes them towards the flames. The mountain guide is easily recognisable by his indifference, the dull way he has of simply being there, like the rock on which he sits. The others are intruders, grotesque figures, scientists. One of them is lying down, his foot resting on a bag.

The cave was not a cave, merely a rift filled with shade by the angle of the sun and with the promise of glory by our overheated minds. On the way back, Peter, ignoring our protests, insisted on climbing a rock wall with his bare hands to examine a vein of quartzite. When he reached it, he found himself face to face with a scorpion: a dead one, although Peter didn't realise that and instantly let go. It's not a particularly bad sprain – his ankle is yellow, with a pretty purple whirlwind around the bone – but he will be immobilised for a few days, incapable of helping us.

He can sense my anger. He doesn't dare speak to me now. Even Umberto's stony face shows annoyance. But in a place so far from the world, it is dangerous to add silence to the silence. It could become too heavy, could cave in and suffocate us. Gio passes around the plum alcohol, which loosens our tongues.

The next day, we will mark out the search zone, vaguely defined by the only two constants we possess, thanks to Leucio. One: the cave is located at the base of the glacier. Two: from the entrance, you can see three pyramid-shaped peaks. We spotted them today, but they are visible from a larger zone than we imagined. All the same, they ought to allow us to limit our searches to a section about two hundred metres long, three hundred at worst. Beyond that, we come up against a cliff of ice, the trough of the glacier, too high to correspond to the clues we possess.

After another shot of eau de vie, Peter raises his hand, like a schoolboy asking permission to speak. He ran a simulation before we came here, and the news is good. This type of glacier – at this location, in this climate – should have seen little to no movement during the past century.

'Natürlich, this is pure statistical speculation. This particular glacier might have behaved in a completely different way. And the forces required to move such a mass could easily have blocked the entrance to the cave.'

'So, in fact,' I say with a hint of annoyance, 'you don't know anything for sure.'

'If I was sure of anything, I would be God.'

Suddenly I want to laugh. Peter, with his raised chin, makes me think of a kid from another age, and a red-and-white-checked

54

tablecloth. It's a shame I'm so shy, my friends. If I weren't so shy, I would tell you that story.

I am sometimes clumsy. Surly, hurtful, even stupid. Reserved, cold, mistrustful. Awkward and hopeless. But I am not a bad man. I have the bumbling kindness of bees: sometimes, without meaning to, I sting the hand that approaches me, out of an instinctive fear that it is going to crush me. I would like you to know that.

'We know that, Stan-*eh*. We know.'

Damn that eau de vie for loosening my tongue.

I was the last one to go to bed. I stayed for a moment outside my tent, comfortably enveloped in the same blackness as the previous night. I couldn't see a thing and it was fine like that. There was nothing *to* see, in any case, nothing but the grey mountains that metalled the horizon.

Then the clouds suddenly parted to reveal a vast, washed sky. The moon was full, but the beauty was not to be found there, distant and galactic. It was close by, on the slopes that surrounded me. The entire cirque was adorned with hundreds and hundreds of silver ribbons, strewn over ridges, sliding down hills, as if the whole landscape were dressed for a village fete. Those ribbons were little brooks and streams descending from the mountaintops, anonymous gurgles that, further down, in distant valleys, would be named by men, if they made it that far. They were still tiny, fearful things, hidden in the grass. Some would die of evaporation, some would become lost, while others would disappear down thirsty throats. The strongest would join forces, sweeping across continents, making oceans rise. I hadn't paid attention to them during the day. But the moon made them glorious, and I noticed to my surprise that one of them ran only two metres from my tent. I dipped my hand into the water. It bit my fingers with a sound of childish laughter before continuing on its way.

The knife moves back and forth across the bread, spreading the good yellow butter.

'Your mother is dead.'

My great-uncle told me the news at breakfast. He came especially from Spain, my mama's homeland.

'You must be brave. You are a man now.'

I was nine.

'It was . . . very sudden. A sort of sickness of the soul. You'll understand when you're older.'

I already understood. Whose soul wasn't sick in my father's house?

We had just returned from two days in Pau. The Commander had taken us to the agricultural fair in the big old cart. *I'd rather shell out on a hotel and keep you where I can see you than have to worry about what you're plotting when my back is turned.*

While he was at the fair, Mama took me to the cinema. Just her and me. It was my first film: *Baron Munchausen's Dream*, directed by Georges Méliès. The people in the audience laughed and yelled, my mother included. I had never seen her like that. Eleven minutes of happiness.

'Look, Stan! A giant insect! And there's a dragon! Look, Stan, an elephant in glasses!'

Yes, it's true, there was already a dragon in this story. But I didn't care about the dragon. Nor about the elephant in glasses. I wasn't looking at them; I was looking at *her*, in the stutters of light and dust that splashed against the canvas. She had put her make-up on in secret, just after the Commander's departure that morning. She looked like an actress.

Even today, for me, *Baron Munchausen's Dream* is an eleven-minute close-up on my mother's face.

Mama had American eyes. She was the one who said that, when I asked her where their colour came from. She was right. Those hinterlands where I would lose myself, those starry canyons, were not from here. She said she had seen whales, waves as high as bell towers, flowers that swallowed bees. The Commander had forbidden her to tell such lies – there were no whales in Spain – and had, above all, told her to keep her damn mouth shut while we were eating, in the rare moments that we spent together. He didn't see the secret looks she shot me, my eyes voyaging in hers; he didn't see a thing. He just burped contentedly as I explored America.

After the movie, Mama took me to a restaurant: a real one, with tablecloths. At home, she seldom left her room because of her migraines, and I had rarely spent this much time with her.

'Choose whatever you want, Stanino. My Nino.'

I didn't dare get much because the Commander had forbidden us to spend money. If I ordered an *île flottante*, I would undoubtedly get a beating. I was going to have to make a choice.

'One day, Nino, you'll invite me to dinner. Won't you?'

'Yes, Mama.'

'You'll invite me to stay with you in Paris. Say it.'

'I'll invite you to Paris.'

'When you're a . . . what is it again?'

'A palaeontologist.'

'That's it, a palaeontologist. You'll invite me to stay with you in Paris, in your beautiful apartment with mouldings.'

'And the Commander?'

'Would you want him to come?'

I mumbled no, my mouth full of *île flottante*.

'Then I'll come on my own. We won't tell him anything.'

'What are mouldings?'

'They're like a prettier kind of ceiling beam. You'll be married, perhaps to a girl like you, who loves fossils. It's important for the two of you to love the same things. I'll have my own room. I'll be able to leave my belongings there. Maybe I'll even live there all the time, if that's okay? You wouldn't mind?'

'No, we wouldn't mind at all.'

Mama spoke in a loud voice because she was Spanish, but that was not why everyone in the restaurant was looking at her. As I've already said, it was because she was beautiful, really beautiful, a redhead whose body was all curves, like a flamenco dancer. I'd heard the seasonal workers muttering *leyenda* as they watched her out of the corners of their eyes and mimicked her swaying hips. Even though we didn't speak much Spanish at home – the Commander thought it a language of farm workers – I understood. *Legend*.

'You'll take me to the opera. I used to adore going when I was a little girl.'

'In Spain?'

'No, in Buenos Aires.'

That was how I came to discover that my mother wasn't Spanish, that she actually came from America. Not that it changed anything. People continued to call her the Spaniard all her life. All her life . . . In other words, the few days that remained to her before she was struck down by that sickness of the soul.

'We'll go to the opera, the two of us; it'll be raining and we'll have umbrellas. One each. Afterwards, you'll take me out to dinner. We'll have oysters. You'll hold my arm because I'll be old. It will be late. You'll go into the restaurant first, because that's what you do when you're a gentleman, and you'll ask if they're still serving. And do you know what they'll say?'

'No.'

'Of course, monsieur, for a customer like you.'

One week. We move our search zone towards the upper part of the glacier. One week and not even a hint of progress. So much time wasted clearing snow and examining rock, ignoring fatigue and bad news. Gio discovers that it is possible to see the three peaks from the *other* side of the glacier, to the north. We have as much work ahead of us as we did when we first arrived. Breath, damned breath which runs out. And so much time, time wasted in despairing. The thick yellow air that does not let us breathe.

One evening, back at the camp, Gio absent-mindedly juggles a woollen sweater knotted in a ball. He kicks it towards Peter, who is still limping. Peter uses his good foot to send it to Umberto, who passes it to me. The ball of wool spins. Gio breaks the rhythm, sending it over Peter's head, and suddenly we are all kids again, rushing after the ball, pass it to me, to me. Something is happening. Umberto lines up a shot, kicks the ball at a tent. Celebrates with the invisible crowd. Peter hobbles outside the tent, dribbles past Umberto, who rolls to the ground screaming. Peter passes the ball, Stan hits a clumsy shot between two bags on the ground, and Gio makes an incredible save. The crowd rises to its feet, a roar of marmots and the wind in the grass. We collapse, out of breath, happy for the first time. A soccer game at the top of a mountain.

Cutting, scratching, hammering.

August unfolds in silence. Gio helps with our searches now. We listen to the glacier, a doctor listening to a patient's heart. If I were the mountain, I wouldn't want people walking on me, repeatedly stabbing me with sharp metal implements. I am afraid that it will seek vengeance.

Cutting, scratching, hammering. Exploring the smallest crack, just in case. Returning, I glimpse our camp clinging like a barnacle to the body of the mountain. In recent days, the landscape has changed spectacularly. The green of the grass has turned to yellow. Each blade cries out to the sky at the injustice of this. Gio anxiously watches the horizon – he knows that, sooner or later, the sky will answer the call of the grass.

Cutting, scratching, hammering. We are close to being worn down when Yuri arrives.

Yuri, the fifth member of our expedition. Yuri, whom I mistook for someone harmless. He appeared from nowhere several days after us, impeccable in his military uniform. Yuri and his exile's accent. Yuri, Peter's friend, who smooths his handsome black moustache when he speaks. Yuri who rolls his r's, who rolls all his letters in fact.

'I was a priest in Bolivia, my friends, an assassin in Mexico, a star dancer at the Scala, a shoemaker in Paris, a king in the land of the pygmies. As for my last job, I'll let you guess . . . Anyone? Did you ever hear about Céleste, the famous transvestite from Berlin? Well, yes, that was me. The darling of the city's cabarets.'

Yuri is well known for his imitations. He offers us a demonstration, a private recital. Ladies and gentlemen, Marlene Dietrich.

'*Sag mir Adieu . . . Dürr wird das Gras, Glück is wie Glas . . .*'

His voice is disturbing, well-modulated, almost feminine. Credible despite the moustache. We applaud, an easy audience, still stunned by his sudden appearance.

'You see, my dear friends, the Reds did not appreciate my opposition to the revolution. I abandoned everything in Russia: my lands, my family. Even today, they are hunting me. They wish to make an example of me. So I change cities, identities, genders. In

Berlin, I was sold by a bastard to whom I owed money. I met Peter as I was escaping over the rooftops. You should have seen his face when I came through his skylight!'

Peter is a ventriloquist of genius. He gives life to his puppet with such conviction that his story sometimes strikes me as more credible than Leucio's. I even thought I could guess that Yuri's preferences were not for women.

I am too serious, without a doubt. Ever since childhood, I have classified everything. True things, false things, things that sting, things that burn, things that are funny and things that are dangerous, things that hurt and console; you have to know about everything if you hope to survive. Yuri is dizzying; he jumps from one pigeonhole to another, he overturns everything like a deranged puppy, messing up the order of the world. This morning, standing up after putting on my crampons, I was surprised for a brief moment not to see him. I was worried about someone who does not exist! So I couldn't resist: I asked Peter where his puppet came from – pure invention? a real person? – because I had to understand how to classify it. Laughing like Marlene, the German raised his hands and sang: 'Who knows? Who knows?'

Yuri, with his woollen head, has become our final bulwark against fatigue. We call him, he plays hard to get for a while, and then he emerges from Peter's bag to a round of applause. Last night, he turned to Umberto: 'What did your mother give you to eat when you were a boy? Sicily?'

Umberto laughs like an organ toccata. Gio's eyes wrinkle slightly. Even I, the too-serious boy, chuckle heartily.

An atheist giant in love with a goddess. A seminarian turned ventriloquist. A guide who speaks the forgotten language of mountains. If I'd known these three when I was younger, perhaps I wouldn't have grown up with a trilobite as my only friend.

The battle raged on the other side of the wall. Armies clashed – my mother against the Commander – and surely they had to be armies to make so much noise, to clash so loudly. Head buried under the pillow, I imagined the scene: the little soldiers scattered across their bedroom floor, the dying cavalrymen, the archers crushed by charging horses. Later I learned that this particular game was played without soldiers.

One day, the police rang the doorbell. The Commander opened the door; he often went hunting with the captain, who looked embarrassed at being there. They spoke in low voices. The Commander invited the captain and his men inside for a drink. With the threat of snow, there was no harm in warming up a little, was there, guys?

I walked around the table with the bottle of eau de vie, taking care not to knock anything over. The glasses disappeared into the men's giant hands, swollen by strength and pride. The Commander pointed at the door: *okay, clear off now*.

One hour later, the policemen re-emerged, laughing. The captain in his handsome uniform nodded at me. I hate uniforms.

After they left, the Commander sat me down at the end of the living-room table. It was the table reserved for important occasions, such as Christmas lunch or counting money. He was enthroned on the other side of the tablecloth, reigning supreme over an ocean of red and white checks.

'How old are you?'

'Six.'

'So you're old enough to know that what happens in the family stays in the family. Right?'

I nodded. It was important always to nod whenever the Commander said 'Right?' He leaned forward and stared at me.

'You wouldn't have blabbed to anyone, would you? A teacher at the school? That damn priest?'

'No.'

'I mean, we're good people. Maybe not perfect. Nobody is. Sometimes people bump into things. Three bruises are of no interest to anyone, as long as they're just bruises, you understand? It was the same for my father, the same for my grandfather, and it'll be the same for your children. That's just how it is in the Pires Aínés.'

He stood up to get more alcohol and sat down close to me. Large blue veins showed through the flesh of his neck. He pinched my arm with his thick fingers.

'You're such a weakling! But one day you'll be strong. As strong as your old man. You'd like that, wouldn't you? So you could push the cart? You'd like that, right?'

'Yes.'

'You want to arm-wrestle?'

'No.'

'Come on. Try to hold out longer than you did last time. Hook your thumb around like that. And tense your muscles before the contact, you understand? Otherwise any little bastard could beat you. One, two . . .'

He smashed my arm against the table.

'I don't believe it, damn it! Are you stupid? What did I just say? You didn't even resist! All right, let's try it again. And stop blubbering. Hook your thumb . . .'

He kept talking, but I wasn't listening. My mind had escaped out of the window; it was running through the night to join Pépin as he prowled, Pépin my king, my puppy drunk on apples, my twilight guardian.

Twenty-first day. Nothing on the southern side of the glacier, where we had hoped to find the cave. Nothing on most of the opposite side, from where Leucio's three peaks could also be seen.

The sun sets. We return to the camp, strides shortened by fatigue. There are only about twelve metres left to explore – a day's work. The cave *has* to be there. When I think back to my naïve desire not to find it too quickly, I want to slap myself.

The prospect of failure increases the tension, and Yuri has a field day. A remark here, an allusion there . . . nobody is spared. Umberto is still mocked for his size, Gio for his enigmatic maxims. Peter does not escape his attacks – Yuri constantly asks why he doesn't have a girlfriend. I don't know whether to be terrified or amused by the spectacle of Peter mocking himself in his doll's voice.

That evening, Yuri tugs pensively at his moustache as he stares at me over our fire.

'Dear Stanislas, since we must think about the future, I would like to discuss a new project with you. I have it from a reliable source – the six-year-old nephew of my second cousin Boris – that Santa Claus lives at the North Pole. How would you like to help me find him? It's your speciality, isn't it, that type of expedition?'

If the others had laughed, I would have done the same. But Umberto looks down, embarrassed. My plate goes flying. My lentils go flying and so does my share of the rabbit killed earlier that day by Gio (everybody got some meat, even Yuri). *Go fuck yourselves.*

I plunge into the night. Behind me, a deathly silence. I won't return until the others are all asleep, because I am ashamed. Because this anger isn't me. It is an ancestral curse, the ugliness of the old man that runs through my veins, poisoning me.

What are the odds that we will find the cave, after three weeks of searching, in the very last patch of rock wall? I can hardly blame my friends for doubting me. Even Christ had St Thomas. Yes, I know: poor old Stan thinks he's the Messiah. But just tell me *one* big discovery that everybody believed in. The telephone? Aviation, perhaps? Give me the name of *one* great man who was understood in his own time. Giordano Bruno? Burned alive. Mozart? His corpse tossed into a pauper's grave. And yet the Earth turns. And yet, the Requiem.

Let Yuri mock me, let him humiliate me. Let men abandon me, let them hang, draw and quarter me, let them crucify me. Let them laugh, let them bury me without ceremony, let them spit my name in the dust.

And yet.

Fifteenth of August. The long-dreaded storm has finally broken. We lose a whole day's work to it – it's impossible, in weather like this, to even think of leaving the tents. I am almost grateful to the elements for giving me an extra twenty-four hours of hope. The storm also gave us our first sight of our guide losing his temper. After walking around the camp in the pouring rain, he ordered us to get rid of all our remaining metal objects. At first, Peter refused to lose the few coins in his pockets. I thought Gio was about to hit him, and I guess Peter must have thought so too, because he quickly threw a handful of lire into the rain. That jingling copper saved his life. At that very moment, the air filled with a smell of ozone and the hairs on our arms stood up. Lightning struck. An electric finger lit up the coins in mid-air and the sky exploded with thunderous laughter, amused by the ease of this particular clay-pigeon shoot. Peter fainted.

I had never seen a storm like it. There were some big ones in our village when I was young, but they worked off so much of their rage on their way down from the Pyrenees that by the time they reached us they were exhausted. They made a big noise, and people pretended to be frightened, but that was all. Whereas here . . . Here, we are inside the cauldron where storms stew. Today I learned that a storm has a taste, a taste of metal and stone that coats your tongue with zinc.

The rain falls incessantly, deep into the night. The treetops glimmer and vanish. The storm remodels the landscape with electric slashes under a bruise-coloured sky. I think about the kid who got lost nearly eighty years before, running away from a storm just like this one. I imagine him discovering a gigantic fossil, a tail as long as the street where he was born, a neck that could reach to the clouds. He can barely breathe, he has never been so scared in his life. So he calls the creature 'dragon', because even a dragon is better than nothingness. Now they can talk to each other, tell their stories. The rain will stop falling eventually.

This boy does not yet know that one day he will leave his village, his family, his friends, that he will wander for a long time, like me. Nor does he know that he will die far from his loved ones, that he will close his eyes for the last time in a room that smells of drains, in a city so hard that he could leave no imprint on it. He doesn't know any of this and it's better that way.

The dawn shakes me gently, in my tent sagging under the weight of condensation. What happened? There is something inside me that wasn't there before. A calm certainty, a tingling in my fingertips. I sense now, with that intuition too clear to be merely human, that we are close to our goal. I had told the others I felt no doubt, but I confess now that this is not true. I was just putting a brave face on my fear.

The air is as clear as water. At the end of the plateau, the rising sun lacquers the glacier like a racing car, *rosso corsa* under a bleu de

France sky. My brook, which had dried up, has now reappeared. It is a real little stream now, an adolescent. Its voice is deeper, even if it still tinkles childishly sometimes when it splashes against a stone. I surrender my face for an instant to its joyous welcome, and then — without bothering to dry myself — run to wake my friends.

The next time the dawn shakes me, I will not open my eyes. It's a trap. The dawn lies to the people it wakes – to the businessman, to the lover, to the student, to the prisoner on death row and, yes, to the palaeontologist too. It fills us with hope only so it can disappoint us more thoroughly. The dusk, older and wiser by a day, taught me this lesson: I was naïve ever to believe the dawn's promises.

Ten hours. That's how long it took us, today, to complete our search. There is no cave in this combe. No dragon either. Just as there is no pot of gold at the end of the rainbow, nor any affection in the hearts of fathers. Nothing but feet stumbling at the end of dead legs. We walk back to the camp in single file for the last time. Gio has gone ahead to light the fire; night is already falling.

As soon as we reach the base of the glacier, Peter comes up alongside me. If he has come to apologise for the other night, there is no point. When he picks up his doll, Peter sometimes loses himself, is sucked back into his childhood. I can't criticise him; I almost drowned in mine. It abandoned me, half dead, fighting to breathe, at the edge of adulthood.

'About Yuri . . .'

'Forget it, Peter.'

'I met him at the seminary.'

Peter has not come to apologise.

'You would have liked him. Yuri always said that man's destiny was to leave. That those who never leave never find the treasure.

And that's what he ended up doing. He was crazy . . . He was crazy and he was my friend.'

I take a deep breath, letting the night enter my lungs before slowly sending it back to itself.

'Why are you telling me this?'

'*Es ist nür eine Geschichte*. It's just a story.'

All is calm.

'What made you leave the seminary?'

'I wanted a change.'

'Peter. About the other night . . . I overreacted.'

'*Ich verstehe*. Yuri can be annoying sometimes. The real one was too.'

Peter vanishes, absorbed by the darkness. Behind me, my companions' footsteps scrape on the schist. Far ahead there is a spark; it wavers, grows, becomes a flame and meets another; they dance, get married, create a large yellow family, reassuring, with many children. Gio has started our fire.

Man's destiny is to leave. If only it were so simple. I could have told Yuri that some men leave and do not find any treasure. Not everyone is like the Capolungo cousin. Not everyone can make it in Hollywood. Not everyone can discover a dragon.

The immediate disappointment is one thing. But my sadness comes from further back. It comes from the boy who, one day, decided to become a palaeontologist. Not for the chance of adventure. Not for fame or glory – although I'd have settled for those. Not for the recognition of my peers. Not even for wealth. No, I became a palaeontologist because I love stories. To tell them, to myself and to others.

I really thought this would be a good story.

My companions eat in silence. Peter has enough tact not to invite our expedition's phantom fifth member; Yuri remains at the bottom of his bag. The young German looks thoughtful. I push the words through the night.

'We'll break camp tomorrow.'

Nobody reacts. Gio pokes the fire, his eyes in the flames. His life is here, in the country of nothing. For him, whether we go back tomorrow or in ten years, it hardly matters. Umberto remains impassive, but several times during the last three weeks I have seen him stealing glances at the photograph of his fiancée. I think he is impatient to see her again, if that adjective can really be applied to a palaeontologist.

Only Peter moves. An incongruous detail: his beard is the only one not to have grown. While our faces have become forests of hair, his faint orange down provoked a barbed remark from Yuri the previous week: 'I've known women with more hair on their butts!'

Peter chews his lips. His head sways from right to left.

'Unless,' he declares suddenly.

Normally this type of comment ends on an open note, three little dots that tickle the listener into asking a question. Unless what? But Peter's sentence ended with a full stop, brutal and conclusive, as if he were reluctant to say anything else. For the first time since I have known him, his expression of permanent exaltation has given way to anxiety.

'Unless our glacier is a statistical aberration,' he says after a long minute of silence.

'In what way?' Umberto asks in a pedantic tone that reminds me he is Peter's thesis supervisor.

'What if — and this is just a hypothesis — what if this glacier evolved in the opposite way to the norm for the period? What if, instead of stagnating or even moving backwards, it continued to grow?'

With a stick, Peter starts to draw in the layer of ashes that surrounds our fire.

'This is the split in the glacier, where we ended our search. This rift could be due to the conjunction of heavy precipitation and the orientation of the slope. A succession of particularly rough winters would have quickly advanced the glacial line of equilibrium. And hot summers, which often follow cold winters, would have delayed the close-off.'

'And in layman's language?'

Geology and glaciology have always bored me, even though they are essential to my job. What I love are living things. Even if those things have been dead for a hundred million years.

Peter starts talking as if to a child: 'Imagine that our glacier advanced much further than we thought. So quickly that it broke under its own weight, because the lower layers did not have time to solidify. That would mean . . .'

'That we were searching too low down. Eighty years ago, the glacier would have been much higher than today! Of course!'

I strangle Peter in a hug; he reacts with embarrassed laughter and the stiff limbs of a scarecrow.

'Once again, I would remind you that this is a working hypothesis based on the possibility of a statistical aberration. In other words, it's probably madness. But as the weather should be fine for another two or three weeks . . .'

What do the others think? Umberto? His big head nods like a rock about to fall from a mountainside. Gio? He shrugs. Even though I have never heard him speak a word of Italian or French, he seems to understand everything we say. I raise an imaginary glass, because the kid deserves it – and because we finished the plum eau de vie two days ago.

'To madness, then. And to Peter!'

I take a shot of pure air and the German blushes with pleasure. I'm not naïve: our chances are still slim to none. But I am grateful for this respite, the firing squad lowering their rifles after a last-minute reprieve that everyone knows will later be withdrawn. Who can blame the condemned man for wanting to spend a few days longer in his cell?

And perhaps this was what needed to happen. Perhaps my dream had to flicker, had to almost go out, before something big could occur.

A childhood memory. An old sheet, salvaged from the scrapheap, hung between the table and the chairs in the living room: my fairy-tale castle, an impenetrable fortress at the top of the world. The essential thing was to believe in it.

Believe in it. But first we had to scale the blue cliff that gave access to the upper part of the glacier, thirty metres above. Fate was smiling upon us: the wall on which the ice was leaning was, at the point where it had broken, sculpted into natural steps. We carried ice axes and ropes as a precaution.

Believe in it. The new search zone is barely a hundred metres long, if we wish to keep the three peaks in our field of vision. In this area, the glacier is not mixed up with the rock. It runs alongside it disdainfully, and any stone that dares to resist it is atomised into rock flour. It is a chaos of seracs, of blocks of ice as big as houses. Same glacier, but a different world. We become even more cautious.

And still we believe.

For five days.

And all for nothing.

Nothing but a threadbare dream.

So let us surrender to realism. Time to give up. We must bow down to whatever is stronger than us; my trilobite taught me that. Time to curl up and sleep, for a long time, perhaps for ever. Leaning against the rock wall, I bite into a fresh apple. At this altitude, where everything is mineral, its flesh reminds me of a forgotten world of roundness, softness. For the first time, the prospect of going home does not strike me as unbearable. Even if it signifies failure, the mocking face of the university vice chancellor when I beg him to give me back my basement office, the great explorer with nothing to show for his adventure but hands splintered with rock. I close my eyes.

'Attention! What do you think you're doing, prrrrivate? Sleeping during guard duty? Thrrrrree days in solitary!'

Yuri rolls his letters and his button eyes with disapproval. This is the first time he has appeared beyond the circle where we light the fire. Peter has brought the puppet along to raise morale. But today, even Umberto is gloomy. The German becomes embroiled in a whispered argument with his alter ego, in one last attempt to amuse us.

'Can't you see that you're disturbing these eminent scientists during their lunch break, you idiot?'

'Do *I* eat lunch?'

'You don't have a stomach, you moth-eaten dummy!'

'Say that again . . .'

The two start fighting. Yuri bites Peter's nose; Peter pulls Yuri's hair.

Four adults halfway up a mountain, and one of them is fighting with a doll. Peter has a genius for the absurd.

'Yuri's earring! It fell!'

Yuri wore a gold ring in his ear; I had only noticed this recently. Peter looks panic-stricken. And since he is digging without having taken Yuri off his left hand, the spectacle gives the surreal impression that human and marionette are searching together.

'Got it! I found it . . . I found it . . .'

Suddenly, Umberto pushes his assistant out of the way and begins digging in the same spot. For a second I wonder if the sun, beating down on us hour after hour, has not actually sent us insane. Umberto dusts off the snow with the same supernatural gentleness that characterised all his work, almost flake by flake. My old friend turns to me with a triumphant smile, a pianoforte keyboard with a note missing.

And then I see it. Under the powder is a layer of smooth, transparent ice like a window, revealing, ten metres below the surface, a wide opening in the rock wall. Gio comes over to take a look and, with an unusual display of enthusiasm, scratches the corner of his eye.

I see some kids sitting in a circle on the mildewed floor of a Parisian cellar, drinking in the words of a man who, without them, was nothing – nothing but the old caretaker who took out the rubbish. Now he becomes a magician, a master of shadows, transforming the sad walls into Cambrian landscapes. Old Leucio was a palaeontologist of genius.

'It is a cave. But that doesn't mean it's ours.'

Behind a startlingly transparent window of ice, we see a prism with a square base, shoved in there by the glacier to guard the entrance. According to Peter, this block should not be here. It is extremely dense, typical of the depths where the close-off takes place: the expulsion of oxygen bubbles from the ice. The only explanation for its presence, and for the glacier's extraordinary vertical and horizontal movement, would be a seismic event. An earthquake, Umberto agrees, nodding. 'Which would also explain the breaking of the glacier: the 1887 earthquake in Liguria. And if it's not that one,' the *professore* continues, 'there are numerous, little-known rifts running through these valleys, which could easily shake the earth while men sleep.'

'Did you hear what I said?' Peter says in a louder voice. 'It's *a* cave . . .'

'Yeah, yeah, they heard you all the way to Turin. Doesn't mean it's ours.'

Peter is right. Natural phenomena such as this are so violent that the layman can hardly even comprehend them; they are beyond the human mind's scope, like geological time or astral distances. Our cave is just a small tear in the fabric pulled back and forth by giants fighting over the planet. All the same, the cavity is there, more or less where we hoped to find it, and while it is impossible to be certain that it's the right one, it is equally impossible to be certain that it isn't.

But the question of access remains. Back at the camp, a check of our equipment confirms that we do not have the necessary tools to dig to such a depth. We have only one real pickaxe, so we will have to use ice axes. We will drill a vertical tunnel, one metre wide and about ten metres deep, directly above the entrance. This will enable us to slide into the cave, presuming that the cave itself is not filled with ice. According to Peter again, this is improbable. The block of ice that has closed the entrance has surely prevented it filling up. In fact, from the surface, its opening appears completely black and empty.

To our surprise, Gio stands up. Usually our guide speaks without any preliminaries, not even a simple throat-clearing, saying what he has to say as soon as there is a brief pause in the conversation, before Umberto once again starts holding forth. I ready myself for a Gio special, one of those maxims so often parodied by Yuri, delivered in his wonderful patois, which seems to imbue his every word with some ancestral wisdom. Instead, in a hard voice, he announces: '*Doa setemanes.*'

Two weeks. September is approaching, and we all know what Gio means. Beyond those two weeks, it is impossible to predict what the weather will be like. On this quiet night, I understand. Autumn is prowling at the edge of the plateau. Gio can sense it. He knows that the coming season has sniffed out our presence here. I feel as if I can perceive its cold breath, a hint of snow in the soft texture of summer, touching us lightly, sizing us up. The countdown has begun. Because autumn, at this altitude, is nothing like autumn down in the plains. It is not a simple narrowing of summer, a gentle curve into slowly shortened days and duvets retrieved from cupboards. Here, autumn is a beast of flesh and claws. As for winter . . . well, nobody knows what winter is like in this theatre of stone. Anyone who might have come here to witness it never returned, or else they kept the secret.

Umberto and Gio converse in low voices for a while, and then my friend translates: 'We have about a fortnight. Maybe a little more, maybe a little less. At the first sign of snow, we will leave. Gio will give the order and we will obey without argument. Our bags have to be kept packed, ready to go at any moment. The camp will stay here and we can use it again next year if we have to come back, or it will be taken down as soon as the plateau is accessible again at the end of spring. Understood?'

We are at the nexus where the winds meet, Umberto explained to me just before we went to bed. That is what makes this region so volatile, its storms so fearsome. At the start of autumn, the Greek (our name for the tramontane wind) crashes into the sides of the mistral. The mistral is not the fastest learner, and somehow it is always taken by surprise. This year, as every year, its reaction is the same: it rears up with a roar like a wounded animal and bites the Greek on the neck, then pins it to the ground to punish it for its impudence. Drawn against their will into this battle, the seasons become confused. Sometimes summer lazes around until October; sometimes it snows in August.

I have a better understanding of Gio's tension now. Umberto has just told me that he lost his son fifteen years ago in a neighbouring valley, on the Italian side. Carlo was guiding a group of English climbers when the snow surprised them. One of the Englishmen went back down the mountain. The others, convinced that it was just a meteorological blip, insisted on continuing. Refusing to abandon his clients, Carlo went with them, and they vanished without trace. They belong to the mountain now, like so many others before them. Is that why Gio spends his life here? Is this some endless pilgrimage for his lost son? Or does he secretly hope that the mountains will one day return his son's body to him? That an early thaw will deposit him by the side of a path, asleep on his side in his outmoded clothes?

Umberto walks away to relieve himself in the night. I turn my back on him and examine the camp. Gio is bent over the fire, his head tilted slightly to one side, as if listening. Can he hear, in the crackling of the wood, the voices of oracles to which I am deaf? The more time I spend with this man, the more he impresses me. He is full of an absence of desire. I wish my sleep could be like his, a dead slumber from which I would arise resuscitated every morning in time for breakfast. Unless I'm idealising him, of course. Perhaps his dreams are peopled with the face of his son, sleeping softly in the Giotto gold of dawn, a handful of minutes from the life-saving sun.

On the other side of the flames, Peter is bent over his marionette. He is sewing it up, his lips curved in a half-smile. I can hear him singing a lullaby, the melody carried to my ears by gusts of wind. It is a peaceful, familiar scene. After a month together in this hostile world, we have become a family. A real family, full of disagreements and misunderstandings.

'Berti?'

Behind me, Umberto is returning with that light tread that throws everyone off balance, even the stones under his feet.

'Yes?'

I nod towards Peter, who is combing his doll's hair.

'He's kind of strange, isn't he?'

'Stan-*eh*, Stan-*eh* . . . What happened to your sense of humour?'

'I never had a sense of humour. You know that as well as I do.'

'Some people smoke, others ride bikes or do crosswords . . . Peter has his puppet.'

'I'd prefer it if he smoked.'

'*Tranquillo.* He's a very good researcher. And he's only twenty-nine.'

'So he's not a kid any more. Why does he act like one?'

Umberto smiles strangely. 'Why? Because he's in love.'

'She'll wait for him.'

'With you.'

I hear the Commander laughing, hear him bellow mockingly as he talked about those men who didn't like girls, and what he would do to them if he ever caught one, and if Stan is a pillow-biter with his fossil obsession, if Stan is a pansy, a faggot, an uphill gardener, then it is time to quickly cure him of that affliction . . .

'You mean he's . . .'

'I don't know what he is, *non m'importa*. I'm talking about intellectual love. Peter admires you. I told him so much about you that he was dying to meet you. He just wants to impress you.'

'What did you tell him?'

'The truth. That you're an angel half the time, a bastard the rest of the time, and the best palaeontologist I know.'

'If he wants to impress me, he's going the wrong way about it.'

'And I suppose you always go the right way about it when you want to impress someone?'

That was when I thought about Mathilde.

Mathilde came every year, like many of those children who swelled the population of our village in summer, because their parents had a house there or because they wanted to breathe our beautiful air. We all wandered around the dusty streets in a loose band, a nebula whose centre was formed around the most popular kids. I was on the periphery, an insignificant comet, following them around sometimes without being noticed, pretending to join in their games.

At that age, all girls are pretty. But she was the prettiest. And finally, after four summers, at the age of thirteen, I worked up the nerve to speak to her. I deviated from my usual orbit and approached the sun, inviting her to come and see my fossil collection, on the hilltop near the little church of Notre-Dame des Lavandes. I couldn't invite her to the farm, because of the Commander.

I didn't expect her to say yes. Girls who were much less pretty than she had already rejected me. When she agreed, my head exploded with incredulity at her stunning beauty and I shrugged and muttered: 'Ciao, see you tomorrow then.' I ran home. I was burning to tell someone. But who? My mother was no longer there.

The next day, I arrived an hour early. I sat amid the scent of lavender, laid out my fossils on a beach towel, folded the edges, and waited. She arrived late. Without apologising, she sat down next to me. We didn't say anything for a long time, so long that the shadow of a cypress tree moved, creaking, until it covered us.

So I unfolded my towel and showed her my ammonites, my

belemnites, and my crowning glory – an insect preserved in a drop of amber. Ignoring them, she turned to me and unbuttoned the top half of her dress. Gaping, I stared at her breasts. They were small and very white, with blue veins and pink nipples. I thought my heart was going to burst.

'What are you waiting for?' she asked with a smile.

I lowered my eyes and stared into the earth. I no longer understood what we were doing there, or the strange emotions that were bubbling up inside me. I started to name each fossil in a trembling voice. She shrugged, said, 'Suit yourself,' buttoned up her dress, and turned away from me.

I'm sorry, Mathilde, it wasn't easy for me to know what to do. Nobody had ever taught me to touch the living. The only flesh I knew was stone. I wished I could explain this to her but I couldn't find the words. It took me years to find them. Besides, I wouldn't have had time. Just then, the boys from the group came pouring out of the woods. I don't know if they'd followed her or if they had come that way by chance. They looked at me as if seeing me for the first time. I heard one of them say: 'Who's that?' Yelling, they swooped on my fossils. They left Mathilde alone because they respected her, admired her. They must all have been wondering how a guy like me had ended up alone with a girl like her near the church. There was an English kid among them, a big boy who came every summer. He pointed at me and shouted, 'Fossil Boy!' The nickname stuck. They called me Fossil Boy until I was eighteen, when a scholarship allowed me to leave the village for good. That afternoon, though, they went berserk. They picked up my fossils and threw them down the hill. I spent months looking for them after that; I never abandoned them, but I only found one. I gradually created a new collection of fossils, and pretended to believe that it was the same.

I am ashamed that I didn't fight them, that I just curled up in a ball and waited for the storm to pass. But the worst thing is . . . While they were throwing away my childhood, laughing and shouting, I turned to look at Mathilde, and I saw pity in her eyes.

Let me tell you something, Mathilde, something I should have said a long time ago. Go to hell, and take your pity with you.

For two days I attack the ice, my face whipped by cold sparks at each crack of the ice axe or the pickaxe. For two days my body vibrates, my tendons strain, my bones crumble. My muscles burn, sing, tense . . . then suddenly stretch out, holding each other back so that they don't give way as I lift the axe again, bring it down in an arc onto the hard ice. With each impact, I leave a little of myself behind.

If I ignore the pain, if I push myself beyond what I thought possible, it is because I have spent the last five years dreaming of what I will see when I enter that cave. I have imagined the moment a thousand times, I have sculpted it, perfected it; I have woven a skein of clouds at dusk, and I think that everything is ready. I will enter, then, at sunset. First I will glimpse the head. It will be held to the side in a patient gesture, a dog waiting for its master. The head alone will be enough to tell me what kind of dinosaur it is – the precise species, ultimately, doesn't really matter. The rest of the beast will be hidden by the darkness. I will move towards it, lamp raised, afraid to discover that the skeleton ends there, after a few solid brown vertebrae. But Leucio wasn't a liar, and the skeleton will bloom in the beam of light thrown by my lamp. Careful not to trip over its feet, I will keep walking until I reach the very end of its tail. There, I will turn around. The head will have disappeared into the blackness, thirty or thirty-five metres away.

As I have already said, I am a humble storyteller who suffers from a curse: I am voiceless, because I have never had an audience to

whom I could tell my stories. I have been voiceless since childhood.
But listen up, all of you.

This animal will give me back my voice.

Third day of digging. Yesterday Gio forced us to stay in the camp for forty-eight hours on the pretext that I had fallen twice. Fatigue, in the mountains, is more dangerous than incompetence or misfortune. We used the time to order our belongings, take stock of our provisions, sharpen our tools.

Getting dressed this morning, I looked down and was surprised to discover that my stomach was almost flat. I couldn't believe it: I have not been in this kind of shape for nearly twenty years. My skin is brown, tight against my muscles. I have dried out like the meat that we eat every day.

Aside from our rest period and the time that we were confined to our tents during the big storm, we have followed the same unchanging schedule since our arrival more than a month ago. Get up at dawn. One hour later, we are on the glacier. We work until nine, when we take a short break to eat some dried fruit, then we work again until eleven. Lunch, and a quick nap, leaning against the rock wall. The glacier is cast into shadow early in the afternoon and we work hard until four, when we make our way back to camp. We eat dinner around six, and go to bed when the stars appear.

Our aim: to excavate at least one metre of ice each day. At that rate, we will penetrate the cave in early September. Every hour gained could be decisive, because I still nurture the hope that we will be able to detach the head and organise its transportation – assuming Leucio's dragon really is there.

At the end of the third day, we put down our ice axes. Autumn is chewing the backs of our necks, prowling under a cold wind, still too young to be really dangerous. Breathless, we contemplate the well we have dug in the ice. It should be three metres deep by now.

It is barely thirty centimetres.

It's over. We won't succeed. We have known it since the first blows of the pickaxe against the ice, but we have continued anyway, driven on by the senseless hope that the nature of the ice might change, that we might reach a softer layer or that, one morning, we might suddenly find ourselves blessed with superhuman strength. But the ice has not changed. And neither have we.

It is hard to imagine that four men armed with sharp metal tools and the force of their rage should be able to penetrate only thirty centimetres into a block of ice in three days of solid work. This ice is incredibly dense, shot upwards from the bowels of the glacier by a telluric convulsion. It gives way atom by atom to the bite of the ice axes; it is ground to dust without ever cracking. It would be wrong to see this struggle as a conflict between two materials, metal and water. The forces at work are far more powerful. The might of the entire glacier, two hundred metres deep at this spot, against the will of four madmen. A wave of cold pushes us back, freezes our breath, our limbs, our minds. If we don't immediately sweep away the powder that we make of the ice, it solidifies again almost instantly. This glacier radiates cold like a negative sun.

It's a quick calculation. At this rate, it would take us nearly a hundred days to reach the cave. Even if we had that much time, this tempo is unsustainable. We have fought like heroes. We all deserve state funerals.

And this is a kind of death. Without photographs, without evidence, I will not be able to finance a second expedition. Even if I persuaded the Commander to lend me an advance, I doubt I would be able to get the money in time. Poor Stan, he's losing it, the gods laugh up above. That old bastard would never give him a centime;

he'd rather die than help his son. Well then, Stan will just have to find the money somewhere else!

But what hope is there that a secret thirty metres long will remain a secret for much longer? A beast like this is bound to arouse covetous thoughts. Someone will talk. Not Gio, obviously. Umberto, perhaps, by accident. Or Peter, boasting. Someone will talk. By the time I return, it will be too late.

Stan staggers like a drunken man on the path back to the camp.

'Why don't you smell of strawberry?'

I stared at the Commander, my throat too tight to swallow. His right eye quivered. I was only eight, but I already knew what that sign meant: it was a precursor of the blows to come, the lashes of the leather belt.

'Did you go to the village?'

I nodded.

'You went to the village because the fair is on?'

I nodded.

'Why don't you speak? Cat got your tongue?'

'No.'

'So answer me. Did you go to the fair?'

'Yes.'

'And you wanted to eat some candy floss. That's what you told me, right?'

'Yes.'

'I gave you the coin so you could buy candy floss. Ten centimes. Right?'

'Yes.'

'Was it nice?'

'Very nice.'

'Bloody gypsies, say what you like about them, but they know how to make candy floss, don't they? You smell of strawberry for about ten kilometres after you've eaten some!'

The Commander leaned gently towards me and asked in a soft

voice: 'So why don't you smell of strawberry?'

'I washed my face before I came ho—'

The slap knocked me against the sideboard. The taste of blood on my lips. A taste I knew well, much better than the taste of strawberry.

'Sit down. Let's try again.'

I told him everything. I had used my coin to buy the herbal gels that the pharmacist made for Mama, the ones that made her better. The Commander had forbidden her to spend his money on such quack remedies. He had even threatened to beat up the pharmacist *and* Mama, so obviously the whole operation was top secret. Or had been.

He looked at me with an expression on his face that I never saw again: compassion.

'If you hadn't changed your story, I would have believed you. Next time, when you lie, keep lying until the end.'

It had never happened before. And I would probably have sworn, under torture, that it could never happen. Impossible. Unthinkable. I had argued with Umberto.

I was idly wandering around while Gio made dinner. My footsteps took me towards the triangular tent that served as our storeroom. Wood, tools, ropes, eight large red jerrycans. *Eight large red jerrycans*. How had I not thought of it before? Eight times fifty. Four hundred litres of oil, as thick as syrup, almost reluctant to be set on fire. When it did finally burn – I had seen it, in our lamps – it let itself be consumed slowly, grudgingly, drop by drop. This oil was the elementary twin of our ice, its alchemical opposite.

I gathered the group and asked for silence. Breathless from the altitude and my excitement, I explained my plan. Fire. The element that changed the destiny of humankind could certainly alter our own destiny, which is so small in comparison. Beginning with the fuse – the hole that we had dug – we would melt the ice by setting fire to the oil. Drum roll, applause, my son is a genius, don't you think, my mother told anyone who would listen. Madame Mitzler came close to believing it too, because she couldn't pronounce 'palaeontologist'.

My companions looked baffled.

'Why not? Hmm . . . but wouldn't it be better to wait until next year, Stan-*eh*?'

'I've been waiting fifty-two years for this!'

'We could come back with more men. Better tools.'

'What better tool is there than fire?'

'Fire? Maybe. Except that this oil is crude. It's a dirty solution.'

'Clean or dirty, who cares? The ends justify the means. And let me remind you that you are being paid for this, and paid well.'

I immediately regretted my words. Gio shook his head in response to some internal dialogue. Peter followed our exchange without a word. Deep down, I knew what was happening. Everyone was exhausted, maybe even Gio, whose movements had grown slower and heavier in recent days. I had, in my euphoria, forgotten about the health of my friends.

Umberto spoke again, looking up at me from below.

'Even if we burned that oil, there's no guarantee that there'd be enough of it. Or that we'd be finished before the snow came.'

Umberto wanted to go home, after more than a month away from the world; I could tell. This expedition was *my* dream, *my* project; he wasn't interested in glory. And anyway, what glory? His name in parentheses, a footnote in an article devoted to me? The money didn't matter to him either. He would probably have come for nothing, for the pleasure of seeing me.

'You're right, Berti. All I ask is that you give my idea a chance. Just one.'

Peter watched for Umberto's reaction, his chin raised like a dog waiting for its master's signal. With a pang, I realised that Peter was my old Umberto. I had thought that I wouldn't miss anything from that wretched time, but I was wrong.

'So if the experiment hasn't been conclusive by tomorrow evening, we'll give it up?'

'And go home, yes. I promise.'

Thank God Umberto agreed. The adventure could continue, for a few hours at least.

Returning to my tent after counting the jerrycans again, I found my friend waiting for me. I was struck by the long, sad look he gave me.

'*You're* financing all this out of your own pocket. That's why you want to stay, isn't it?'

'Yes. I sold my apartment to cover the costs.'

'The university didn't approve this expedition. It probably doesn't even know about it. You lied to us.'

It's true, Umberto, I lied. I learned as a boy. It's a long story, a story about the taste of strawberry; you wouldn't be interested.

'I'm sorry.'

'So am I, Stan.'

Sighing, he walked away, taking with him the little syllable that he always added to the end of my name, and for the first time I understood that it was a syllable of friendship, a little game between the two of us.

The jerrycans, each one weighing fifty kilos, are too heavy to be quickly transported to the glacier, and we can't risk sacrificing our flasks by using them to decant the oil. With no other containers available to us, we have to empty half a jerrycan onto the ground to lighten the load. In doing so, we lose twenty-five litres of fuel. I hope we won't regret that loss later. The earth drinks up the black pool as Gio stands watching in dismay. It is a stain on his mountain, almost a personal insult.

It may not seem much, twenty-five litres. At this altitude, it is the weight of the world. We stagger to the glacier, each taking turns to carry the container for ten minutes. When we come to the final wall, our guide takes over.

An unpleasant surprise: our hole is fifteen centimetres smaller than it was yesterday afternoon. Incredible. The glacier breathes out the humidity of the air, and uses it to heal itself. It regenerates while we sleep, destroying our efforts to destroy it. But the glacier won't win, I swear. We are too close to give up now.

My burning lungs remind me of our first days here, an eternity ago. But we lack the enthusiasm that drove us then, and the proximity of the cave, in its sarcophagus of ice, does not make a difference. Instead of inspiring us, it makes us despair. I can feel it too, this despondency exhaled by the stone, which contaminates our souls. It is perhaps one of the mountain's self-defence mechanisms. An aroma of melancholy to prevent men lingering here, like those flowers and insects with a smell so foul that predators are repelled. Unless it's actually designed to protect *us*. Time to go home, guys. Or else.

Gio, Umberto and Peter are sitting close to the hole, shapeless figures. My swollen fingers unscrew the lid. Inside the cavity, our twenty-five litres spread and pool, a black sludge, thinned out to the point that it looks more like five litres. I glance at Umberto. We haven't spoken since the previous night's incident. He doesn't smile.

I light a match. And drop it in the puddle of oil.

Victory! My method allowed us to melt fifty centimetres in a day, a result that might appear derisory, and yet it is five times faster than we managed with our ice axes. If we keep up this pace, we will reach the cave in twenty days. Maybe even sooner, if we can improve our technique. The problem is that the oil, as it burns, instantly creates a layer of water between itself and the bottom of the hole. This thin liquid barrier somehow seems to insulate the ice from the flames. Our burning oil floats on a cushion of water without attacking the glacier, and again I am struck by the strange impression of a beast that is protecting itself, adapting to new angles of attack. If we try to remove the water from above, it breaks up the coating of oil into little islands that end up going out, forcing us to waste fuel. By the end of the day, Peter has come up with an ingenious system of channels to drain the water from below. But we will have to constantly maintain it, blocking up the old siphons and creating new ones as the level descends, otherwise the burning oil will disappear down those channels. It's a real conundrum.

The edges of the hole are now a black sludge, a mix of oil, melted ice, and the earth that we bring from the camp on the soles of our boots. When the oil burns, it gives off a thick, heavy, toxic smoke. I feel as if we are desecrating the mountain in pursuit of my prize, like those masters who, failing to inspire obedience in their dogs, resort to punishing them constantly instead of showing patience. Like the Commander. One day, Pépin almost bit his hand off after he punched the poor dog in the face.

I have punched the glacier in the face. I deserve to be bitten. But I don't have a choice. None of this will matter, it will all be forgotten when we reach the cave and find the dragon. Even Umberto seems to have come round to my point of view. This evening, by the fire, I see him raise his flask in a silent toast.

The question does not even arise. We will keep going.

The glacier burns. It twists, it rumbles, it cracks angrily as we torture it. September. Our fire moves like a slow bullet through its body, sending a long smear of black blood towards the surface. The hole is five metres deep now. Its edges are a gangrenous wound, a suppurating circle with a ten-metre radius. We are halfway there. Day by day, we are descending into the dragon's dreams.

Our task has become more complicated in recent days. As we dig, it becomes more and more difficult to remove the meltwater. It's impossible to bail out from a layer of burning oil, so we are forced to take drastic measures: pouring in the smallest amount of oil possible, setting fire to it, and emptying it after barely fifteen minutes even if the oil is still burning. Then we start again. We have to do all this while holding on to large pitons that we have hammered into the wall to create a sort of makeshift ladder. To compensate for this slowdown, we have set up an intermediate camp closer to the glacier. A home-made sled allows us to transport the jerrycans.

Every evening, I carefully clean out the bottom of the hole. This ice haunts us, it is killing us, but my God it is beautiful! After a whole day of fire, all it takes is a few wipes and there it is again, that crystal transparency, just beneath the grime. In the light of the setting sun, I press my nose to the ice and today, for the first time, I saw the inside of the cave. I couldn't see much — just a rock, lit up by a single adventurous beam of sunlight, and only for a second. It touched the stone the way you might tap a kid's nose. But it happened: light penetrated the kingdom of death.

Gio has forced us to take another day of rest. The glacier is there, within reach. All that is missing is black smoke in the air, reassuring me that we are close to our goal. The waiting drives me crazy, even if I can see – in the dark rings around Umberto's eyes, in the clumsiness of our tired movements – that a break is necessary. Each time I hear the glacier crack, I feel as if it is taunting me. It is not a song any more, but the sound of mocking laughter as it regenerates its icy skin, centimetre by centimetre, in our absence.

But the real reason for my anxiety is that I can feel it: the smell of cold as we go to bed, the faint yowl of the beast climbing towards our cirque. Below, in the plain, a leaf has turned red. Nobody down there worries about this, of course. Autumn hunts in the mountains and we are its prey.

Three metres. There are only three metres left to dig. Luckily, the weather is perfect. I can now see the rock inside the cave when the sun lets me, and a pale stain a little further inside. All day long I have to keep cutting short my flights of fancy to concentrate on the work at hand.

With our beards and our black-stained faces, which we hardly even bother to wash any more, we look like miners. Our clothes are so stiff they are starting to crack. Our skin is like bark. Only our limbs remain flexible, lubricated by exercise. But our muscles are suffering, and more and more often they simply give way. We are approaching our limits.

Three metres.

Six days.

It's all we need.

The closer we descend towards the cave, the more our evenings drag. Those hours seem pointless. It is dead time, which we must kill all over again. I went to find Umberto, just before dinner, to apologise. I shouldn't have lied to him – my old friend – about the funding of this expedition. I had my reasons, some good, some less so. He responded graciously, but I found it hard to tell if something between us was broken. I asked him about his fiancée to cheer him up a little. It is painful for me to see how much he misses her. He was supposed to go back for an operation in September – was that why he was so reluctant to prolong our mission? Umberto turned red and admitted that it was a simple teeth-whitening procedure, a little-known technique performed by a dentist friend of his in Milan. He flashed me his piano smile, a little battered and out of tune, and the sight of it touched my heart.

Then it started to snow.

Autumn

A imé was losing his mind.

Aimé the shepherd. When anyone in our village talked about 'the shepherd', it was always him they had in mind, even though there were also Martial, Jean and the others. Martial, Jean and the others didn't mind this. Aimé was old, so old that he was already a shepherd when the Commander was born. That merited respect.

Aimé was losing his mind, people said. This idea terrified me almost as much as wolves. He would come before the summer to take our sheep to mountain pasture. Apparently it was quite a sight, one man surrounded by a white cloud that came up to his waist, slowly advancing up the hillside. But I had never seen it, because I hid whenever he came. At night, I tried to imagine what he might look like, with his brain slowly seeping out of his ears, bits of it blown away by the wind.

One day I felt unwell. Nobody knew what was wrong with me. When the village doctor asked me to describe my symptoms, I explained that there was an emptiness in the world, an absence where before there had been a presence. He stared at me for a long time, rubbing his beard and muttering, 'I see, I see.' Then he announced to my mother that I had a magnesium deficiency.

After a few days, I understood. I hadn't seen Pépin in a long time. Too long.

My dog had disappeared.

We searched for him everywhere. Even the Commander joined in, grumbling. My mother forced him to accompany me to the police station, where we were informed that the authorities had better things to do than look for a dog. The Commander was furious. *I told you, you cretin! You humiliated me in front of the captain!*

My mother explained that Pépin had perhaps dissolved in the wind, that he had escaped his earthly body the way a prisoner escapes a prison. Never again have I felt as lonely as I did that day, not even the day my mother dissolved in the wind.

'It was Mulat-Barbe who took your dog.'

I was sitting snivelling on a split log that served as a bench in front of the farm. I didn't know the man who had spoken to me. He was so old, though, that I immediately realised he must be Aimé. Amid the trauma of Pépin's disappearance, I had forgotten that he was coming to our house to pick up the sheep. I had forgotten to hide. But it turned out that people must have been lying: there was no sign of him losing his mind. Unless he'd already lost every single bit of it . . .

'Who's Mulabarb?' I asked.

He turned his cataract eyes southwards. 'A shepherd, like me. He's a thousand years old, less a day. He was the first shepherd. He took your dog.'

'Why did he do that?'

'Because times change. One world dies and another is born.'

It wasn't this Mulat-Barbe who had taken Pépin. But even if shepherds are crazy, there was some truth in what the old man told me.

About ten years after our first meeting, I came across Aimé again. I was prospecting, a skinny, pimply teenager, in a ravine where I had found a magnificent *Cenoceras lineatum* the previous month. Aimé hadn't changed. That day, I finally understood why people said that he was losing his mind. He didn't know who I was, and neither my name nor my father's sparked the faintest recognition. He just said to me: 'Listen to the mountain.' Then he called his sheep and moved away with them.

Except that there were no sheep. He was alone. For thirty years, the local farmers had pretended to hand over their animals to him and watched him climb up to the mountain pasture. Not encircled by a cloud of wool, as in the old days, back in a time that nobody remembered, but surrounded by nothingness, an absence.

Gio walks ahead, straight into the sun. The narrow path leads us up towards the summit. It only snowed for an hour last night, but I barely recognise the landscape where I have just exhausted six weeks of my life. All the contours have softened. Just a ghost of green shows through when a sun-drenched rock manages to melt the snow. The combe seems less craggy than before, the stone less forbidding: we are leaving this place just as it appears more welcoming. But it's pure illusion. The sun is shining this morning, but the temperature had fallen about fifteen degrees when we woke. Autumn slit summer's throat during the night. Nobody except Gio suspected that it could have crept so close to the camp without raising the alarm.

The expedition is over. I pledged my allegiance to Gio, as did the others. I don't want to pressure them to allow me another reprieve, even if it seems to me that we were so close to succeeding. The sun has burned their eyes and their hands are blistered. They have given me enough.

With the assured rhythm of experienced mountaineers, we zigzag in long slants amid fallen rocks. Two hours later, we reach the peak, the very place where we entered this cirque a month and a half before. Dizziness. This time, though, it is not caused by the abyss beneath our feet, the via ferrata vanishing into the void. No, I have changed without realising it. My vertigo is no longer vertical, it is horizontal. I am like the prisoner who is suddenly set free, panicked by the absence of corridors and walls. My gaze, instead of bumping against a barrier of stone, reaches out into infinity. Down there, I see the mountain pass leading to the shepherds' lands, a few clusters of sheep like giant peonies. A dark forest blots the horizon. My imagination takes over, already hurtling down the path that we took to come up here; it rushes along, carried by its momentum, leaping from stone to stone, from root to root, and then there we are at the log bridge, among pines, and then it's the village. And finally the bus, the bus with its pistons clacking, that will take us to the sea, to flat ground, in an odour of grease and old red leather.

A small stream bursts from the rock now and splashes over the bars of the ladder with silver laughter. It is tiny, teasing, tinkling. It wouldn't scare anybody. But it should. It is a glacier waiting to happen. It will end up freezing, Umberto explains, then it will swallow up the via ferrata and transform it into a waterfall of ice. Impassable.

'That's why we have to leave. *Adesso*. Now.'

He turns to me with a compassionate look, and at last I recognise my old friend.

'We'll come back in the spring. I think I can get us some loans in Turin.'

'Thank you, Berti.'

Now that it is all over, now that I have finally accepted my fate and stopped struggling against it, I am at peace. I put my harness on, and I wait for Gio to set foot on the first bar before I tell them the news.

I have decided to stay.

Silence. Stupefaction. Then words are battling, overlapping. Gloves dance furiously in a pantomime of panic. Everyone has something to say, an opinion to share. Their words will change nothing, and I suspect that they know this. So they grow even angrier.

Now they are talking among themselves, too fast for me to understand, Umberto interrupting Gio, Peter wading in, nobody really listening to anybody else because, deep down, they all think the same thing; they just express it in different ways.

'It's madness. Pure madness. Another cold snap like that and you won't be able to come down. Only an experienced mountaineer could get out of that combe, and even then it would be risky. It's out of the question!'

'I need six days, Berti. Maybe less. I'm going to take my chances. It's *my* decision.'

'It's not sensible.'

'I've been sensible all my life. Believe me, it's pointless.'

Gio makes a weary gesture. He utters a few sad words, which Umberto translates: 'Do what you want. Gio is going back down. His contract ends here.'

I understand him completely. The guide nods farewell and disappears into the void. I hold my hand out to Umberto.

'Don't worry. I'm not crazy. If the weather turns, I'll be out of here like that.' I snap my fingers. 'I just want to be sure that I did everything I could. You understand?'

My friend shrugs. He knows me well enough to be certain that

I won't change my mind. And as I don't like long goodbyes, I turn away and leave, just like I left my father's house – without a word – to tattoo my youth upon the world.

Halfway down the slope, I turn around for the first time. I didn't dare do it before this. Three hundred metres above me, Peter and Umberto are coming down after me. At least, now, it is *their* choice. Well, that's what I tell myself anyway; I'm not sure I really believe it. They would follow me into the depths of hell, but could you truly call that a choice? I wait for them, blinking furiously in the sun, the damned sun that makes my eyes water, and then we walk on together, in silence. I want to thank them but I don't know how. Nobody ever taught me. They are saying what they have to say with their feet, so why bother with words?

The snow is starting to melt. Hope is reborn. It is too late to work today. Out of habit, I go to the hole in the glacier while Umberto and Peter unpack their things in the intermediate camp. The end of the tunnel is covered by twenty centimetres of snow, already turning hard. I remove at least half of it.

Most astonishing of all is the effect produced by the night's storm. It has covered up the black mire that surrounds our hole, erasing our insults and giving the impression that the glacier is healing. I feel sick at the thought that I must, the next day, restart our litany of fire, grease and putrid smoke, that I must deepen the wound. To my own surprise, I kneel and place my hand on the behemoth, as if to console it. *Only a few more days,* I promise. I hope that nobody has seen me.

By the fire, Umberto and Peter eat in silence. The air is tense with fatalism, with their blaring resignation. We have done the calculations: we should have enough oil to reach the cave. In Gio's absence, I have decided to take more risks: we will start work earlier and finish later. I am sure we can gain an extra day of work in this way. And at this time of year, that could be the difference between success and failure.

Eyes closed, I breathe in a big mouthful of night and flames, snowflakes and incense. I have not felt this good in a long time. I am at that pivotal moment in a man's life, the cliff edge of insanity, when nobody else believes in him. He can step back from the brink, and everybody will praise him for his wisdom. Or he can make the leap, in the name of his convictions. If he is wrong, he will become a synonym for arrogance and blindness. He will for ever be the man who didn't know when to stop. If he is right, the world will worship his genius and his courage in the face of adversity.

It is the crucial moment when you must no longer believe in anything, or believe in everything.

After school, I vanished into the forest. I was searching for Pépin, without admitting it to myself. I was afraid of finding his dried-out corpse, of discovering him caught in a trap, too late to save him. Perhaps he had called me, called again, long vertical howls that tore through the night like pillars of pain; perhaps, before everything came to an end, he had wondered, in his dog language, why nobody was answering him, why *I* wasn't answering him, after he had done so much for me.

Suddenly I had the fright of my life. Against the dazzling sky, an enormous silhouette darkened the undergrowth. A *wild boar*. I saw myself dead, disembowelled, my mother weeping over my pale body stretched out on the marble slab, the rest of the world indifferent.

But the pain didn't come, and I opened one eye. It wasn't a boar, but an eagle, caught in a bramble. Wings outspread, crucified in mid-air by the vicious thorns, it hovered two metres above the ground, an apparition feathered in gold by the setting sun. Cathedrals had been erected for less than this.

With the aid of my penknife, I cut the creepers that were tangled around its wings. The bird's beak drew blood from my eyebrow, its claws tore at my hands. I ignored the pain and worked with the desperate determination that I should have used to save Pépin. The eagle contracted its body, gathered the last of its strength and, with the beat of one heavy wing, escaped the clutches of the forest.

I collapsed in an odour of iron, dark earth and mushrooms. I felt the call of the meadows rushing under my belly, their breath of hay, the panic of rodents as my shadow passed over them, and for the first time I saw a way of leaving this valley. All I had to do was to fly, to fly towards the sun.

I came to on a carpet of leaves. The Commander was splitting logs as I staggered towards the farm. I could hear each blow echo in the hills. He stood up tall when he saw his son covered in blood. As I walked past him, he smiled proudly and slapped me hard on the back.

'Well done, my boy.'

He imagined that I'd been in a fight at school, and I didn't set him straight. It was something, a father's pride. You could carry it under your jacket and take it with you into the classroom. It was invisible, and it would keep you going all day.

The third week of September. The weather is good and I allow myself a modicum of optimism, just enough not to bring me bad luck. Yes, I'm superstitious. There are still about two metres to go, perhaps a little less, perhaps a little more. We can only estimate the precise distance separating us from the cave. But we are almost there.

When we returned to the camp this evening, Gio was there, rekindling the fire so he could prepare our dinner. He had come back, feet heavy with his duty as a guide. We sat beside him and ate in silence. There was anger in his eyes, maybe even fear, for the first time, though he didn't say a word.

We have worked for two more days. Our fatigue has evaporated, but Gio warns us: it is still there, crouching inside our muscles. It is the mistake of a moment, the kingdom of inattention, the joyful laugh of the void that takes advantage and closes around its prey. Calculate every movement. Question every decision.

We are now only a metre or a metre and a half from the cave. We suffered a small disappointment yesterday: the pale stain that I'd glimpsed inside the cavity was merely a piece of wood, rubbed smooth by water. You can see it very clearly now. I am not discouraged. The darkness behind it is rich with promise. The snow has almost melted and the grass stands tall again, greener than ever. Even Gio has relaxed and so has the atmosphere around him.

Troubled sleep. I wake at dawn, trembling with cold and

impatience. If we work twice as hard, one of us could enter the cave today. Tomorrow, at the latest. I push against the flaps of my tent — they don't move. Only then do I notice the murky light of dawn, the muffled song of the mountain.

I am buried.

We all emerge from our tents at the same time. The snow is up to our chests. It's a strange sight, like a polar morning in Pompei: our torsos floating on an ocean of powder, statues lost at sea. In a single night, the white lava flow has submerged our camp in feline silence. The sky has the texture of chrome.

This time, nobody tries to convince me to go home. Each man is here of his own free will. Each can leave whenever he likes. And as is sometimes the case with mountains, the only way out is up. Not a word is spoken as we equip ourselves for an ordinary day's work and start our journey towards the glacier. Instead of the usual ten minutes, it takes us an hour and a half to get there. Somehow we uncover the rope that guides us there every day, and follow it to its end.

Our tunnel has vanished. And I thought we'd been wounding the mountain! Now I understand how presumptuous that was. The mountain tolerated us the way we might tolerate a mosquito. In the night, it yawned; it had had enough of these stinging little bites.

Gio barks orders. The mechanism is engaged; it runs smoothly. We rope up, we sweep away the snow. Reopen the wound, until it bleeds. The layer of grime reappears, then the edges of the tunnel. The snow has formed a bridge over it, so the hole has not been filled. We drop down to the edge, breathing fast. We have left the oil at the camp, and none of us has enough strength to go back and fetch it. Tomorrow. We will start work again tomorrow. Our dragon has waited several million years; it can wait another day.

Gio describes the signs to us. He lines us up like schoolchildren and explains everything. With this much snow, the rules have changed. Evil lurks, watching us. It could pounce at any moment. More insidious than an avalanche, and just as deadly.

Hypothermia. First stage: peripheral vasoconstriction. Blood drains from your extremities, converging on the organs to protect them from the cold. Symptom: shivering. Who would suspect a little shiver? Second stage: the pulse slows, the supply of oxygen to the brain is reduced. Your judgement is altered; you become confused, sleepy. As soon as we start to feel drowsy, we must call for help, Gio tells us. And the third stage . . .

'You won't even be aware of the third stage. So there's no point scaring you with that. We've wasted enough time.'

Four days pass under a bright mercury sky. It hasn't snowed again, but our progress has slowed even more. We are infuriatingly close to the cave, but we cannot use the oil to melt the ice any more. It has become too difficult to remove it. The tunnel is now so deep that anyone who went down there would suffocate when the oil burned. And as there is only one jerrycan left, our guide forbids us to use it. We must keep it in case of an emergency. As he gives this order, the old Italian stares at me threateningly with his eyes as green as a mountain lake. Disobedience is not an option.

On our knees at the bottom of the hole, we take turns scraping away with the ice axe. Almost ten metres below the surface of the ice, the cold is piercing, breathtaking. A diamond-pure cold. Despite our layers and layers of clothing, despite our hats and gloves, we have to go back up to the sunlight every thirty minutes. While one man digs, another stays on the edge of the hole to keep watch – Gio's strict orders. If the man below stops moving at any point, the watcher must call his name. It's uncomfortable down there: the tunnel is so narrow that it is difficult to crouch. Umberto can no longer descend because he is too big and suffers from sciatica.

We are flotsam, broken shells beached in mid-air. Our bones and muscles and veins all ache. Every time we wake in the morning, we move through the stages of evolution: crawling, slowly rising, holding on to a rock and groaning as we stretch our curved spine. By the time the water for our tea is boiling, we are *Homo erectus*, but to become *Homo sapiens* we must wait a little longer. We struggle to sleep despite our exhaustion. Tempers fray; the tension is constant. Peter, in particular, worries me. He has changed since our return. Several times, he has answered coldly when I have asked him innocuous questions. And when Umberto rebuked his assistant for the loss of one of our ice axes, clumsily dropped into a crevasse, Peter replied that at least he could use an ice axe. The German is nervous. He jumps at the glacier's slightest movement. There are no more puppet shows by the fire.

September is fading away. A thick, unbreakable coating of ice now covers the upper bars of the via ferrata. While the other three might be capable of descending it with the aid of pitons and ropes, it would be very difficult for me. I don't worry about it, not tonight. All my thoughts are focused on the fifty or sixty centimetres of ice still separating us from the dragon of dusk. Because, as I was finishing my shift at the bottom of the tunnel, I felt sure I could see the beast! The earth moved, the sun sent a shaft of light a little deeper inside the cave, and in that moment I glimpsed it, for less than a second: a beautiful white head with patient eyes.

Dozing in the living room, his rifle slung across his lap, so insignificant that he barely showed at the surface of the world, sat the Commander, my father. That night, the wolves had left me in peace and I had gone downstairs to drink from the pump. Or perhaps I was no longer afraid of them.

I approached in silence. A bouquet of flowers was rotting on the sideboard behind him; it had taken my mother's death for him to give her flowers, and he hadn't even thought to put them in water. The room smelled of wine, beef terrine, a hint of sweat. His sun-darkened arms poked out of a wool sweater, those arms that could lift an axe the way I could a pen. His hands hung limply, but I couldn't trust appearances. They were dangerous.

This was one of his habits: cleaning his rifle at night when he came home from the bar. He had been there a lot recently. He said it was out of grief, but he was lying. I had looked the word up in the dictionary at school: *profound distress caused by the loss of a loved one.* I had looked up distress: *emotional pain.* Nowhere in the definitions was there anything about laughing loudly with one's hunting friends at the bar.

Gently I took hold of the gun. The Commander sniffed, moved in his chair, and then started snoring again. The rifle was a beautiful Darne 1906, the apple of his eye. I opened the breech block, picked up two of the twelve cartridges lying next to the soup bowls, loaded the gun, snapped it shut. I knew each step by heart, because he had forced me to learn them. I caressed the metal arabesques, the

117

chocolate-brown wood, the handsome blue barrel – the same blue as my Pépin. So much beauty to cause such destruction. I lifted the rifle. Lined up the rear and front sights on the lower part of his forehead, between the prominent eyebrows and the thick hairline. I did not tremble, or not too much anyway. At the other end of the barrel, the Commander mumbled in his sleep, unsuspecting.

I could tell you that I put the gun down and went back to bed. That would be a lie. I squeezed the trigger. The gun went off and the window behind the Commander exploded. He jumped to his feet and grabbed the rifle from my hands, what the hell are you doing, blinking furiously, his eyes red and black from anger and wine. Sorry, Papa, I just wanted to put it away, I could see that you were asleep, I didn't want to wake you, it went off on its own.

The Commander eyed me doubtfully. He sat down slowly, shrugged, and went back to sleep.

It's hard to kill a man. I know because I tried. Next time, I will steel myself for the recoil.

I'd said it to Umberto – Peter is strange – even if that was not exactly what I believed. With the camp's lack of privacy, I was bound to see him. It was inevitable.

I was coming back from the storeroom. He was rubbing himself with snow behind his tent. He was bare-chested. His arms and his gaunt torso were marked with curved pink and white lines, scars that mapped old terrors. *Self-inflicted violence*, our family doctor would have diagnosed, rubbing his beard. *I see, I see . . . Peter has a magnesium deficiency*. But there is no such thing as self-inflicted violence. It always comes from afar, from outside, no matter whose hand holds the blade in those last few centimetres, until it is touching the skin. I didn't know what demons Peter had tried to exorcise. I could have told him that it was pointless. I knew that all too well. To prove her point that our family had sadness in its veins, my mother slit hers open one day, to let the sadness out. It didn't work. The sadness remained.

Peter froze. He didn't cover up. I continued looking him in the eye. I wanted to say something, to share my own scars with him. To admit to him that, at fifty-two, I still sewed name labels into my sweaters because my mother had once told me that, if I did that, she would always be able to find me.

But, for once, I followed the Commander's advice, repeated every year at every holiday meal, and I kept my big mouth shut. Peter started rubbing himself again, and I walked on.

*

After a long absence, Yuri reappears. Without his moustache. The fashion is for clean-shaven men now, he explains, before recommending that we follow his example. We smile, aware that our faces are being consumed by hair which we hardly even bother to trim any more. Very soon, the sarcastic remarks begin again. He attacks Umberto first. His fiancée must be wondering where he is, doesn't he think? Isn't he scared that she will marry someone else, someone younger and better-looking than him? Someone smaller and lighter, someone less likely to flatten her if he turns over in bed. Umberto laughs, but I can tell that each remark is eroding his good, big, stone soul.

I hadn't thought about this: we have no way of communicating with the outside world, and we should be home by now. Is Berti's beloved biting her nails, worrying about his absence now that the horizon is white? Not once has he complained about this, or even mentioned it.

This is the essence of Yuri's genius. Deep down, it is me he is attacking now, relentlessly: this expedition, my vision, my stubbornness. *Look carefully, Stan. Look at our faces and our hands. Look in our eyes and our hearts. You don't see anything? Exactly. And it's all your fault.*

The woollen monster is right. We have been living on top of one another, twenty-four hours a day, for almost two months. As in the army, there is no privacy or modesty here. Yet I don't feel as if I deserve such persecution. High on self-importance, Yuri has stopped paying attention to his audience. He no longer listens out for the shadow of anger in the laughter he provokes, is no longer aware of the lines he is crossing.

The mood shifts. His face crumpled, Yuri suddenly tells us the story of a group of lumberjacks who went to work in Siberia in the dead of winter. They didn't come back that night, nor the next day. *Vanished!* Yuri moves his hands like a magician's. Two weeks later, a rescue team found their naked corpses scattered around the remains of their camp. Some of them were mutilated. What demon had they enraged in the snowy forest? Yuri asks in a whisper, his flannel gaze moving from face to face.

Gio shakes his head and laughs mockingly. Peter puts his puppet down. He looks annoyed.

'That's a *true* story. It was in the papers. I'm not making this up.'

A shrug. A burst of patois.

Umberto: 'It might be true, but it's no mystery.'

'Those guys were half naked in minus-forty temperatures!'

Yes, this is the third stage of hypothermia. The one that Gio spared us. *Paradoxical undressing*. The muscles relax and the blood is suddenly pumped towards the periphery of the body. A feeling of intense heat. Your temperature falls to twenty-eight degrees and you start stripping off. You are simultaneously burning up and dying of cold. Welcome to the kingdom of hallucinations, the great opium dreams of the comatose. By this point, it is already too late. The mind has drifted too far from itself to have any hope of returning.

'And the mutilations? You're not telling me that's from the cold!'

'Predators. Scavengers. Foxes, crows . . . Those are the only demons worth worrying about.'

That evening, Peter goes to bed without wishing us goodnight.

Our circumstances are difficult enough already without Yuri's barbs or macabre stories. I try to reason with Peter, as calmly as I can, the next morning as we are heading towards the glacier.

'Your knowledge is precious to us. And I appreciate your presence, truly . . . But we have to stay together. We need all our concentration, and I just feel that your marionette—'

'I can't control what Yuri says. Sorry.'

I've had enough of his eccentricities. 'You think this is all some game?'

'No. It's hell. And given that I agreed to stay here to help you, my dear Stan, I think the least you can do is to be polite to Yuri.'

I stab a finger into his chest. Any harder and I would have knocked him over.

'Nobody forced you to come back. Nobody forced you to stay.'

Peter opens his mouth and his gaze slides towards Umberto like a mechanical mouse. He shrugs.

'No. Nobody.'

He lowers his head and drives forward into the cold air, step after step, along a never-ending path.

An argument with Peter, an argument with Umberto, both of them pointless. Stiff fingers that drop tools, shaky legs and bodies that veer clumsily into other bodies, sorry, excuse me, just be careful for God's sake, you spilled the water that took thirty minutes to boil, I told you I was sorry what else do you want me to say, okay okay everybody calm down I know we're all tired but, damn right we're tired, we're tired of this wild goose chase you took us on, if it's a wild goose chase why don't you just leave, I'm not forcing you to stay here, no no I know, I didn't mean it like that, and still Gio is silent; that's all he ever is. We calm down a little bit, we ignore one another, we pass the ice axe with eyes averted, then after a while it starts again, it's inevitable, be careful Jesus you got snow on my shoes, really you're kidding there's snow on a mountain? And on it goes, a northern funeral march accompanied by the creaks and snaps of the glacier.

I should have remembered that I was capable of killing.

Only two more days and we will enter the cave. Gio told me that the weather should remain fine, he's sure of it. We will go back home happy or unhappy, rich or poor. But at least we will *know*.

Tonight our fire is a regular inferno, a farewell to the mountain. The intermediate camp has been taken down, and we are back at the base camp in readiness for our departure. Gio has spent the last two days hammering pitons and tying ropes down the waterfall of ice that covers the first bars of the via ferrata. With his help, I hope to be able to descend it. If not . . .

If not, nothing. There's no point even thinking about it. Feeling distant, I try to remind myself how this all began. I can't enter the cave without the enthusiasm that brought me here: that would be sacrilege, like walking naked into a cathedral. What was the name of the little girl who told me about Leucio's dragon? I don't even know if I can remember her name. Louise? Juliette? It was five years ago. A long time.

'You know, Stan, in the army, I knew lots of senior officers.'

Yuri looks me up and down, stuck on top of Peter's left hand. I will never know how the German manages to give his puppet such a variety of expressions. With one three-fingered hand, Yuri scratches his cheek while continuing to examine me thoughtfully. His high-pitched voice rises from his little body while Peter's lips remain perfectly immobile.

'And I have to admit – even if we don't always see eye to eye, you and I – that you make an excellent general.'

I have turned away, but now I look back at the marionette, thrown off balance by this compliment.

'A model general, oh yes. The foot soldiers do all the fighting and you collect the medals.'

This is the moment when I make my mistake, the one Gio has been warning us about for a long time. I could try to pin the blame for this on exhaustion, the chemistry of our bodies, or some evil spirit prowling around the edges of the fire, but really it makes no difference. The net result is that I jump to my feet and charge at Peter.

He gets up too. He stumbles as he takes a step back, but catches himself. On his face I see a child's terror, an unfathomable dread that stops me in my tracks. Then, as has often been the case in recent days, there is a glimmer of defiance in his eyes. He raises his trembling fists, his childish fists that weren't ready for an adult adventure and were too afraid to say so.

I can't hit him. So in my anger I tear Yuri off his left hand and throw him in the fire.

The puppet lands in the middle of the flames. Peter cries out like a wounded animal. He tries to throw himself after it, but Gio and Umberto hold him back. We are burning oil tonight, not wood, and the flames would stick to his skin if he got too close. The marionette immediately goes up in a ball of fire. I see Yuri's eyes run, his hair transformed to an incandescent halo that quickly spreads to his body. He is gone in less than a minute.

Gio and Umberto let go of Peter. He stares at each of us in turn, with so much emotion that I can no longer tell if he is in shock or filled with hate. His gaze rests on me and I tense, ready to fight.

Then he breaks down in tears. He cries and cries. I have never seen anyone cry like that in my life, not even my mother: snot gushing, shoulders convulsing. His suffering silences the night. He kneels down close to the fire and lifts his head to look at me, his birdlike head that weighs a ton.

'I didn't leave the seminary . . .'

'Sorry?'

'They sent us away . . . Yuri and me.'

'Peter . . .'

'You're just like them. You burn what you don't understand.'

I dare not look at the others. I go to my tent, blowing as hard as I can on the embers of my anger. Peter pushed me too far. He deserved it. Right?

It takes me a long time to fall asleep. Outside, the cold creaks, attempting to insinuate itself inside through the smallest of openings. In the middle of the night, a cotton-wool silence falls. It is snowing. For once, this news makes me feel relieved. There's nothing like fresh snow to wipe the slate clean, to erase our clumsy drawings and our chalk smears, our miscalculations and our dunce's caps. When day breaks, we will be able to start again.

P eter is not at breakfast when I leave my tent the next morning. Umberto is bent over his tea, Gio is smoking near the fire. With a movement of his chin, Umberto replies to my silent question. Out there on the glacier, still wet with fresh sunlight, a black dot is moving. Peter went to work without us. He is following the rope, alone, through a metre of snow. No easy task.

'Better not,' says Umberto, when I start getting ready. 'You stay here. I'll talk to him.'

Talking won't change anything, I want to reply. It's just something priests do to fill the oak silence of confession. But instead I say nothing and put down my bag.

Gio and I have finished the preparations for our departure. We have unwound and rewound the ropes, then done it again because I got mine in a tangle. We have checked the moorings of the tents that will stay here until our return next spring. The time is close. Turning towards the glacier, I look out for a clue, a sign that the cave is finally open, that the last few centimetres of ice have given way at last beneath our ice axes.

Umberto! He is hurtling along the rope. He slips, disappears into the whiteness, then gets up again and runs towards us, waving his arms. I can't breathe. My feet, heavy with snow and anxiety, refuse to move. Finally, Umberto's voice adds sound to his gesticulating silhouette, to this giant figure that for once appears tiny. *Aiuto. Aiuto.*

Gio has already set off, a rope around his shoulders. He runs towards Umberto. *Aiuto. Help.* I follow him. Gio passes Umberto without slowing down and continues running towards the glacier. My friend falls to his knees in the snow, wheezing whitely. His teeth are bared to the air, trying to snatch oxygen, that rare silver dust that we share every day. He talks and talks in Italian. He doesn't understand that I don't understand. He just keeps jabbering away.

But the words don't really matter. I know that expression. It's the one reserved for disasters, the look on the face of the person who tells you about your mother, your beautiful blue dog, people that you love, or others that you don't know but who were loved by someone.

Umberto does not know. Peter came out of the hole and walked a few steps to eat some dried fruit in the sun. They nodded to each other. A minute later, Peter had vanished, just like that. There was nothing left but a handful of fruit scattered over the ice at the edge of a crevasse: an apricot, a raisin, a glove, and that was all. Umberto has no idea what happened.

There was nothing Gio could do. He rappelled down the crevasse. He had to use pitons and add a length of rope to penetrate its depths, descending towards the centre of the world where blue turned to black. We waited on the surface in silence. When he came up, he shook his head. I yelled at him to go back down. We couldn't abandon Peter like that, so easily. Perhaps he was waiting for us, like Pépin in a trap, like the eagle in that bramble, waiting for us to come and free him, waiting . . .

'That's enough.'

Umberto spoke without looking at me. The rift is too deep. The mountain has taken its revenge.

Peter is dead. There are not a thousand ways of saying it. In fact, there's just one. The same banal, clichéd phrases, worn almost soft from being used so often, breathed over grey faces or in the doorways of rooms closed too long to the light of day. He died for his country.

He died of this, he died of that. He died for no reason. Whatever. He's definitely dead. We have to repeat these words. Even if we already know, we don't believe it, because the reasons are never good enough. So I force myself to expel them, to spit them into the cold. Nobody listens but someone, somewhere, will need to believe them.

Peter is dead.

I blame all this whiteness, this snowy whiteness that drives us crazy and leads men and animals astray. Even though I know a prism would reveal the colours hiding within it, even though I tell myself repeatedly that this whiteness is a larval rainbow, I cannot forgive it. I am guilty. Yes, guilty of believing that we could stand up to it.

Sky burial, cremation, interment. Birds of prey, fire, earth. We are palaeontologists. We are aware of all these rituals invented by men to say farewell to their dead, to prevent the living from following them into the underworld.

In this country of bone and cold, in this no man's land, how should we say farewell to Peter? Our minuscule population, our society of three, does not know the answer. In the absence of a past, we must invent everything. We are palaeontologists and that fact is no use to us at all any more.

We have gathered his belongings at the edge of the crevasse. Fragments of Mass come to my mind, Lavernhe's soft pouting mouth spouting Latin phrases as if they were sports results at my mother's funeral: *mors stupebit et natura, Étoile de France won the French championship by beating Red Star, cum resurget creatura, by a score of three goals to one, stand straight for God's sake*, hisses the Commander, smacking me on the back of the head because my legs are wobbling, but what do you expect, I'm nine and a half and I've been standing in this cold church for over an hour. Sorry, Mama, Peter, I'm sorry, look, I'm standing straight. *Mea culpa, mea maxima culpa.*

I tell myself that a thousand marionettes are burning in the world at this instant without a single ventriloquist dying, but it doesn't help:

I blame myself for spending two months with a man and knowing nothing about him, or knowing him too late, *and that is why I implore the Virgin Mary, the angels and all the saints — and you too, my brothers — to pray for me, the Lord our God, amen.*

Stan will now read from the Bible for his mama, announces Lavernhe. I look at Umberto: he's just spoken, he's asked me something. *No, Father, I can't read now, I just can't.* My head is full of *Dies Irae*s and Kyries, but I gasp silent clouds, strange dry sobs. My sadness is always the same — it hasn't changed in forty years: a wounded animal tearing at my stomach in a blind panic, desperate to be free, but becoming more entangled as it writhes and convulses, preventing me from releasing it into the light of day that will kill it at last. *Come on*, the Commander says, blowing into his hands, *enough of all this, lads, let's have a drink to warm us up.*

We push Peter's belongings. They fall down the abyss without touching the sides and suddenly he is no longer there, no longer there at all.

Peter laughed. Peter irritated. Peter sang Marlene Dietrich. *Sag mir Adieu.*

Their bags are ready. My friends have gone as far as they can. I don't try to hold them back. They don't ask me to accompany them.

Gio stands in front of me, putting on his harness in silence. He clips and unclips the snap hook on an imaginary rope: he is showing me the precise movements I must make when I find the rope that he will leave behind on the ice waterfall, enabling me to reach the uncovered part of the via ferrata.

Together, we walk to the edge of the slope. Heavy footsteps, slumped shoulders. We shake hands one last time. Umberto stops before starting the climb. One look is enough. *You're sure? You understand that if you can't make it down on your own, no one will come to help you? That each day reduces your chances of survival?*

Yes, Berti, I know.

They go up slowly, two black sticks of charcoal moving across the whiteness without leaving a mark upon it. They vanish behind a rise, then reappear, tiny on the summit. I imagine that Umberto waves to me and I do the same. Perhaps he imagines my wave. Then they flicker briefly and turn into sky.

I return to the glacier the next day and I dig and dig as if my life depends on it. Well, it's true: my life does depend on it. I force myself to maintain the discipline of the previous days: to go back up every hour, before the fatal tiredness descends. On the first day, I pierce thirty centimetres of ice.

That night, loneliness grips me. The day Umberto and Gio left me, I was so tired when I got back to the camp that I fell asleep without eating. But now, in front of the fire, I become aware of what it is to be truly alone. A *physical* pressure. The air pushing down on me, crushing me. The entire universe conspiring to make me feel how useless and insignificant I am. A hand on my face, forcing me into silence, making it hard to breathe. You might tell me that it is possible to be lonely in a crowd, but you know nothing. I dream of crowds. People shoving me, treading on my toes, bodies packed together on rush-hour metro trains. I am surrounded by millions and millions of cubic metres, acres, tons of nothingness, void, absence. If I fall, nobody will pick me up. If I fall asleep, nobody will wake me. That is what it means to be alone.

I take refuge in my tent and pray for the sun to rise.

At dawn, I start work. I have to finish it, and get out of here. Is it October yet? I have stopped counting. I lift my eyes to the circle of dazzling sky, ten metres above my head. Noon. Only a few more blows with the ice axe. Deep inside my kingdom of cobalt, I hear the glacier sing more clearly than ever. It becomes mingled with Peter's voice, Marlene in a dead body. I scrape, I hit, I sweep away the broken ice. A ghostly choir. Don't listen. I hit and scrape and sweep again.

That's it. I've done it. When I reach out with my hand, there is no longer any obstacle between the cave and me.

It takes me another two hours to clear a passage wide enough. In my excitement, I forget to go back up and I fall asleep. I owe my life to my ice axe: slipping from my fingers, it drops, point first, into my tibia. The pain wakes me and I hoist myself up, like a cotton worm in my soaked clothes, towards the light. Abbé Lavernhe was right – the light saves man when all seems lost – even if he said it on the day of the annual soccer game against Buzy, when the sun blinded their goalkeeper, allowing our team to score a last-minute equaliser.

But yes, the sun. It sets, just as I imagined it. I didn't do it deliberately – it was a gift of chance. At this depth, though, its rays are no longer enough. I crawl, lamp first, towards that sanctuary I have sought for so long. My flame enlarges the cave. The orange light pushes back the darkness. There is a pile of driftwood near the entrance, enormous and white. I have the strange sensation that I am walking at the bottom of the ocean.

I stop suddenly. I am wasting this moment, searching this place as if it were a cellar and I was looking for a lost tool. I should do things properly. So I close my eyes and think of Leucio. I think of my mother and I think of Mathilde. I think of Pépin, of Madame Mitzler, of Marsh, of Deller, even of the Commander. Lastly, I think of the members of this expedition, the living and the dead.

When I open my eyes, I see it there, its empty sockets staring at me. Finally the shock wears off, and I burst out laughing.

Three days after my friends' departure, I climb up to the via ferrata. Behind the mountain peaks is a backdrop of purple clouds so thick and ominous that they look like a theatre set. It is madness to attempt the descent with such clouds in the sky. But waiting would be even madder.

I found Leucio's dragon. I found it sleeping on an ocean of driftwood, looking a little sad. It was not a brontosaurus. It was not an apatosaurus or a diplodocus. It wasn't a dinosaur at all, but a very big reindeer or moose. Ancient, undoubtedly, and proof that there really was life on this plateau, at least at the time of the last glaciation. I understood instantly how Leucio, a frightened kid with a fever, might have mistaken it for a dragon. The pile of white wood on which its head rested must have given him the impression of a gigantic skeleton. Poor Leucio, how scared he must have been. Poor Stan, what an idiot.

This caribou skull is from the end of the Pleistocene. It is perhaps ten thousand years old. For a layperson, it is a treasure. For a palaeontologist, no more than a curiosity. This type of discovery is not rare. It's an amusing punchline, and one day I will laugh about it. A few decades from now.

Standing above the via ferrata, I harness myself, my mind elsewhere. One week ago, the view from this point floored me. The green, the brown, the red roof of a distant cabin lacerated my retinas after weeks of greyness. Today, all is white. The snow levels everything, erasing the differences of altitude with one grand autocratic sweep. My eyes whisper to my feet to take a step forward, promising them that an open plain stretches out ahead, that what they will meet is terra firma, not a 300-metre fall. Thankfully, Gio trained us well. Another Stan checks each gesture, each movement, keeping me alive.

Snap hook in hand, I am ready, when a wall of blackness strikes me down, a mental vertigo that throws me backwards into the snow. I don't know what to do. I don't know what to do with this snap hook, with this rope that is steeped in the clouds. Yet I saw Gio showing me each action; I can see it all again, even now. The problem is that his hands are a blur. All I remember are his eyes, like mountain lakes.

Over, under . . . I try various combinations. I invent my own knots. It's no good. I do not understand by what mysterious interlacing this hunk of metal and this length of hemp can be connected to keep a human being alive. Even less how I ever imagined I would be able to do – alone, without any experience – what others take years to learn.

On all fours in the snow, I crawl away from the edge and stare at the combe, which stretches out in front of me, the place from where I came. I have not wept in a long time. I did not weep when my mother died. Not because I didn't want to: on the contrary, my head was full of burning water eager to spurt out of my eyes. But the Commander glared at me, and I didn't want to *act like a queer* in front of him.

At last I weep for the immense waste that I have caused, for the kid taken by the glacier, for the friendship worn thin by the mountain, for those damn ropes and my useless hands. I weep for madness too, the madness that gripped me, for reasons that don't really matter. I wanted to believe in a fairy tale. Well, now I'm trapped in one: I am going to have to live in a castle of ice until it melts and I am freed.

Winter

I wouldn't have done it if it weren't for that thing with the inheritance: the papers I had to sign in person at the notary's office, some story about a forgotten bank account in my mother's homeland. I had to spend a night in the monster's lair. I had to see the Commander again. This was ten years ago. It was our last meeting.

I hadn't gone back since leaving the village. A farm doesn't change, and I arrived during a white winter that looked just like all the other white winters I had known. I knocked at the door. No answer. The workshop was empty, and so was the barn. I pushed open the large wooden door.

'Papa?'

The inside smelled of oldness. Old stones and old men. The house was as silent as a cold hearth. It stirred memories of soup and heartburn.

'Papa?'

He was lying in the living room, an overturned pedestal table at his feet, surrounded by my mother's collection of cherubs, all smashed to pieces. He pushed me away when I tried to help him up. My damn joints, he muttered. He didn't say hello, and I didn't ask him how long he had been lying there like that in his porcelain purgatory, his limbs stiff with gout and misplaced pride. He dragged himself over to the living-room table and sat down. The tablecloth was the same, but the ocean of red and white checks had become a puddle. Everything looked tiny, the ceiling loomed low. He poured himself a glass, smacked himself on the forehead, took a second glass and filled it to the brim before pushing it towards me.

So, my son, how are you? Tell me about your life. I miss you. I was talking about you just yesterday.

'You remember the Castaings boy? Well, he took over his father's farm. They're going to expand it. It's going really well.'

I miss you too, Papa. You should clean up a bit. Maybe you should hire someone to help you. I'm going to visit more often.

'I'm a university lecturer in Paris.'

I knew you'd go far, my boy. I'm proud of you.

'And what does a university lecturer do, exactly?'

'Research.'

'What are you searching for that you couldn't find here?'

Twenty years of silence, a silence as deep as an empty water trough in the middle of summer, and we had nothing to pour into it, not a single drop. The Commander pushed back his chair, grimacing, and took another bottle from the dresser. I started to move towards him and he yelled: 'I don't need help, for fuck's sake!'

Suddenly he stopped being old, a wrinkled fogey in his grey sweater. When he sat down again, he was a giant with tree trunks for arms, a juggler of anvils, a brute capable of dancing with that strange delicacy that had seduced my mother under a sky full of fireworks one Bastille Day.

'I sweated blood for years, you know, for you and the Spaniard. And how did you thank me?'

Second glass. I had never seen the Commander drunk. When he hit me, he was always sober.

'Why couldn't you be like everyone else, eh? With your feet planted in the good earth of home. A man who knows his place. And it is a good place, this earth . . .' *Third glass.* 'Where did you get all your fancy ideas about studying, as if we weren't good enough for you? I'd have given you a different kind of education. I'd have told you the truth. Like with your mutt . . .'

'Pépin? What about him?'

'It was your mother who didn't want you to know. I'd have told you the truth, man to man. That dog bit me once too often. And after what happened with the Castaings boy, I didn't want any more trouble. You can't keep an animal like that on a farm, it's dangerous. It was the only thing to do. Behind the stable. Between the eyes. He didn't suffer.'

My jaw trembled. My lips, my eyes, my teeth. I stood up slowly and headed towards the door. In the doorway I turned around for a final goodbye.

'I only regret one thing. I wish I hadn't missed, that night.'

He scratched his stubbly cheek. His skin was too big for him, as if his bones and muscles had shrunk inside it.

'It was the recoil,' he explained with a shrug.

I thought about their first meeting. I rubbed at my parents as if they were made of old copper, to remove the black stains. I lifted their heads, slimmed their bodies, lit up their eyes. They must have loved each other for a moment, when they danced under the paper lanterns on 14 July, unless they stood still while everything else danced around them. Your father was handsome, my mother had told me, and he was gentle, and he danced like a god. I have thought about their first meeting a thousand times, at night mostly, when I felt as if I were suffocating. They must have loved each other. If not, then what reason did I have to exist, to breathe, to take another's place? But where had it gone, that love? I searched for it under my bed, in the cold walls, in the forest, in my mother's eyes, and then in the eyes of other women, and in the end I realised that it had turned to stone. It must have rolled off somewhere, fallen through a hole in a pocket. They might even have searched for it themselves a little bit, but it's so hard to find: one small stone in the rubble of the world.

At the station, waiting for the train to Paris, I was approached by a man whom I didn't recognise at first. He was the former police captain, the one who hadn't wanted to search for Pépin, the Commander's friend. He was coming back from Bordeaux, he told me, where he'd had his gallstones removed. I didn't even know what gallstones were, he said, and suddenly there I was being cut open to have them taken out! He laughed at this so loudly that the stationmaster, dozing at his counter, awoke with a start.

I didn't feel like making conversation with this man, but I forced myself to be polite. Yes, I was a palaeontologist – the captain frowned: *pay-lee-on-tol-oh-jist?* – yes, that's right, it's a sort of doctor, if you like.

'Well anyway, my boy, one thing's for sure: you take after your old man,' he said to me as we were about to separate.

'Sorry?'

'Oh yeah. Well, Henri and me, you know, we were at primary school together. Then he had to drop out of school to work on the farm, after what happened to your grandfather. You remember? Because of the Krauts and all that.'

'I never knew my grandfather.'

'Ah. Well, it was Christmas Eve 1870. The Germans sent him a brand-new grenade as a present. He tried to send it back, right, *nein danke*, and then . . . boom! It went off. He was lucky he only lost an arm. Anyway, when he got home, the teacher went to see your grandparents. She asked them not to take your father out of school: he was better at writing than any of the others, he'd go far, maybe even be a notary's clerk when he grew up . . . That's what I meant when I said you took after him. Henri should have stayed at school, if you want my opinion. Your grandmother thought so too, but your grandfather quickly reminded them that he was the one who wore the trousers. Even with one arm, he knew how to make people respect him. He needed help on the farm, and that was an end to it. Not like now, with all these machines. But Henri, he could have been an intellectual too. Maybe not at your level, but an intellectual for round here, if you know what I mean. The only difference between you and your father is that he was a fighter. And you . . . well, not so much.'

I saw pity in his eyes. Pity for someone incapable of fighting. Then my train arrived. The whistle blew. The 3.14 to Paris is about to depart, ladies and gentlemen, please take your seats . . .

Call me snow: I am no longer anything else. It is everywhere. On the mountains and in the hollows, a flat line covering the peaks. Inside my collar, my shoes, my gloves. In my lungs, my mouth and my eyes. On my eyelashes, in my beard, in my tent. I am nothing but snow now.

The first few weeks were difficult. First there was the euphoria. The euphoria of realising that our provisions of meat and dried fruit, enough for an army, would allow me to survive the winter. Gio had set up the camp in a safe place: there was no danger of being buried under an avalanche. As for the cold, it was bearable. I had almost fifty litres of oil, which I used to light a small fire every evening, burning it sparingly, log by log. I lit it as close to the tent as I dared, and when it started to die down I would go inside and curl myself into a ball around its warmth.

I quickly realised that, in these circumstances, it is the mind that is most in peril. With nothing to distract it, your brain will turn inwards and slowly devour itself. So, every day, I go over my studies, as if revising for an exam. I list the geological periods – Cambrian, Ordovician, Silurian, all the way to the Quaternary – then I divide them into eras (Palaeocene, Eocene, Oligocene) and I date them, juggle the figures, going back and forth, remaking the universe in my head: I create the sun, I shape the Earth, I invent the weather, I give life to the oceans, I separate the continents – Asia here, America there – I cover them with monsters like the one I was looking for, I extinguish them, I walk bent over, I stand straighter, I discover fire,

I forge metal, I build cities, I walk along a yellow corridor to my basement office, I sit down there and fall asleep, exhausted. The next day, I do it all again.

The most difficult thing is the silence. It has snowed, several times. I no longer hear the glacier crack. I no longer hear any birds. There is only the wind, whose rare visits I greet with joy. When it blows from the south, from the lowlands, I close my eyes and reach out with my senses, striving to capture and savour everything that it has brought with it: snatches of conversation, lovers' sighs, store signs creaking, the smell of tar, the ring of a bicycle bell and a Christmas cantata, anything that my imagination can dream up.

I sing a little too, but I avoid talking to myself out loud. I've seen too many sad cases, early in the morning on my way to work, unkempt and muttering incomprehensibly to themselves, wandering around in their own world of snow. I may not look very different from those men, but I refuse to imitate them. I cling to what remains of my dignity.

I often think about Umberto and Gio. Did they make it home safe and sound? Yes, they left before the big storms. Umberto is probably smiling at his fiancée with his big white teeth right now. Perhaps they are already married? The calendar that I keep in a notebook tells me that it's mid-November. For a whole week, every evening inside my tent, I go to his wedding, a party that lasts for ever. In clement weather, on the shores of an Italian lake, we help ourselves to simple dishes, the thought of which makes me salivate: fresh fruit, grilled fish, brioche. Especially the brioche, perhaps with some of the Commander's jam spread on it. That jam is the only thing that might yet save the old man from an eternity in hell. The small amount of kindness that existed within him was exhausted in those jam-making sessions long ago, in a fury of quince, apples and sugar.

I have not returned to the glacier. The way there is too exposed, and several avalanches have already – before my very eyes – swept away our usual path. Besides, what's the point? Our hole has been filled in, our traces erased. Did they even exist, the glacier wonders, or did I just dream about those idiots?

Another day dawns and I reconstruct the world again in order to stay sane.

A blizzard tries to kill me. For two days, the snow is blown across the landscape in whirlwinds, leaving this place unrecognisable. It is impossible to sleep more than three hours in a row without being buried alive. Allowing myself only snatches of sleep, I fight against this circling enemy, this lying dervish that pauses only for the pleasure of starting again. Whatever I do, I must not think about the months that separate me from springtime. I survive one minute. Then the next. *Open wide, Nino, another one, just one more spoonful. It's good for you; your body doesn't have enough magnesium.* I must pinch my nose, swallow the minutes, keep going just a little longer.

My hands are frozen. By some miracle, I managed to light a fire, taking advantage of a lull in the storm. It used up a significant amount of oil. In the light of the flames I checked my fingers, fearfully searching for the black spots of frostbite. I had wrapped strips of cloth around my gloves – they saved my life.

After three days, I collapsed in my tent, too exhausted to struggle any more. I knew that death would be painless. Then the blizzard decided to torment another valley, another country, and I opened my eyes to a sunny morning.

At the bottom of my bag, inside the toiletry bag that I brought with me from Paris, I find a small, broken mirror. It has been several weeks since I have opened it.

I glimpse my reflection. November has whitened my face. No, it's not a face, it's a frosty landscape, broken only by a brown nose and two burning eyes, trapped between an upturned jacket collar and a wool hat pulled down low. My lips are invisible. The cloud stuck to my beard is the only sign of life in this forest, the only suggestion that a man is breathing somewhere deep within it.

According to my calculations, tomorrow will be 1 December. And even if I am wrong by a day or two, it hardly matters. I'm still here, alive. Not bad for a *femneta*, a guy who can't fight, a pansy.

S tan slips away in his handsome black suit. The world is kinder on the other side of the mirror. Hair slicked back, shoes polished. One step forward and everything will be forgotten. The men pacing around the living room, the hands messing up his hair, ruffling it up into spikes that he has to keep flattening. The oak box in the middle of the room – 'Oak! You did things right,' the Commander's neighbour said. The boy from the mirror put his oldest fossil in there, while no one was looking, just before they closed the lid. A trilobite. *Don't just stand there staring at yourself in the mirror like a moron, we'll be late for the church.* They are strong, these men: they lift up the box as if it were empty. Maybe it is empty? The boy didn't check. Maybe his mother has taken off into the hills; he wouldn't blame her. He'd like to do the same, one step forward, *for God's sake, what's wrong with the boy, he's obsessed with that damn mirror!* But he has to stay, he's not big enough. He can't go through it, not yet.

The child from the mirror turns and walks away. One day Stan will leave too. Patience . . .

December flays me. I have never been so cold in my entire life. Each breath is like a thousand white birds with blades for wings. I force myself to eat, methodically. A hunk of tough meat, a piece of dry fruit, a mouthful of water. Several times a day. Over and over again.

Is Umberto worried about me? Does he think I'm dead? I hope he doesn't blame himself for having left me here. He had to go back, to save himself. The world is already far too full of situations where people die for others' madness. And yet, sometimes I am overcome by an irrational rage: why don't they come back and rescue me? What are the villagers doing? I know the answer, of course. I'm just pretending, because it reassures me that I can still get angry. The path that leads to the via ferrata is the kingdom of avalanches, and those people wouldn't come even if one of their own had chosen to brave the elements here, to strand himself on these celestial shores. There is too much respect for madmen in these valleys, for the saints of tomorrow.

M erry Christmas, Nino!
    Is that you, Mama? Hang on, I got you a present. It must be somewhere around here.

Here you are. This nice, round, very white snowball . . . I made it for you. And for tonight, I've prepared a special meal. Dried meat on a slice of dried fruit, followed by a slice of dried fruit on dried meat. And to drink . . . the purest spring water you have ever tasted, collected from the very mouth of the stone where it first emerges into the world. Then we will sing and dance and I will give you your real present. I will give you summer.

I don't remember what I did yesterday. And today, I found myself waist-deep in the snow, at the bottom of the escarpment that leads up to the via ferrata. I don't remember leaving the camp and I have no idea how I got there. All I recall is sweeping the snow outside my tent, as I do every morning, then closing my eyes . . . and when I opened them again I was several hundred metres away. It's the shepherds' disease, the one that old Aimé had. I am frightened.

The New Year has begun. I think I can smell a slight warming in the air, unless it's just my imagination. When will the ice melt? When will I be able to climb down that ladder and leave my prison? I force myself to hope.

I

Will

Survive.

I keep my mind busy, day after day.

I list all the things I love. Dogs. Honey (the clear kind). Colour (any). Trains. September mornings. Mornings in months that don't exist, but that I could invent and who would blame me? The chapels where nobody goes any more, the ones dug into the night by years of patience. Tunnels, and the light that laps at their end. Whales. Silences (plural). And America, of course.

I list all the things I don't love. Silence (singular). The north wind. Cold indifference. Egg yolk. My second toe, which is longer than my first. Egg white. Being ten years old and not having a mother. Being

eleven and not having a mother. Being twelve, thirteen, fifty-two . . .
Time does not heal that wound.

I list the women I have loved . . . No, that's enough lists for today.

Standing in the snow, not far from the via ferrata this time. I must
have walked a good two hours to get here and I have no memory of it
at all. More worryingly, the cold is back, even sharper than before. Its
blue blade cuts through the air at the slightest movement. It slashes
my tent, my clothes, effortlessly.

I have adopted a new routine to restrain my amnesiac ambulations.
Every morning, I force myself to sweep the path that leads to the
escarpment. If it doesn't snow, I sweep the snow on the slope. If
it snows during the night, I start again from the beginning. It is
exhausting, thankless work, but this is the path I will take to leave the
combe. Every gesture is like a glimpse of the future.

I am losing weight. For several days, I am confined to my tent by a
bad cough and a fever. It must be written, in a giant accounts book,
that I have not yet served my time. I wake one morning with my
lungs clear, as weak as a newborn baby. Cured.

February begins. And the cold – the real cold – arrives.

White-out. The phenomenon so feared by mountaineers: the world blown away. The landscape taken by the wind. No more shadows, no more contours, no up or down. Just this infinite white flatness in all directions, the nausea that pins you to the ground, hands clawing the air as you try to climb back to the surface. But the surface of what? Everything is the same, everything is white. Your body spins and whirls, falling endlessly through nothingness. You lie down. You don't move. You wait. Wait for the end of the white-out.

Now I know. I know what winter in the mountains is like. It's a train. A furious machine, a frenzy of sparks dancing on the rails, steel laughter on the horizon. It screams, it rears up, it bumps and jolts as it pulls its cast-iron cargo. Of course I am talking about pure winter, not the cuddly season that touches our existence in the plains and cities every year. I am talking about a voracious god whose anger planes mountaintops and emboldens glaciers. Perched on those peaks, it blows its contempt for all life. It is destruction. It is breathtaking beauty.

There is no question now of sweeping the path every day. The trick worked: it seems to have brought my mind back to itself – no amnesias since I started. But now it is impossible to remain outside my tent longer than ten minutes at a time. And even those ten minutes cost me an hour of uncontrollable shivering afterwards, huddled under my blankets. I am not ashamed to say that I take care of my business inside the tent, in an old bowl whose contents I then throw as far away as I can. I don't mind dying, but I refuse to let them find me in some ditch with my backside in the air.

The wind blows almost every day now. It no longer comes from the south. It is a white, hollow wind, full of angles and sharp edges, and I cling to my soul when it passes. It stops only at night. And what night! It chimes like a crystal glass. Those stars, my God, those stars . . . If I could fall asleep one more time while staring at them, I would be a happy man. I have only five minutes to admire them, between the fire going out and my return to my tent. The blackness comes back then, powdering my cheeks with a shimmering talc. I will miss them, when I get home. It doesn't take much to kill a star. One street lamp is enough.

It's ridiculous, Mathilde. I still love you. All the reason in the world is nothing against a flash of blonde hair. Perhaps we will bump into each other in the middle of a busy boulevard. A little thrill of recognition: *aren't you . . .?* A surge of memory: *yes, remember when we . . .?* And we will start over. You will console me and delight me. I'll be less harsh; I'll have laughter on my lips and the sparkling blue eyes of all invincible lovers. Your hair will be shading into white, your face lined by the years. I won't care. Trees lose their leaves but still the sap is green inside them. A cloud does not alter the sun that it hides. I will follow the paths of your wrinkles. You could never not be beautiful to me.

But of course we won't bump into each other. And I will keep stumbling down paths of ice.

Everything has frozen. I can walk on the snow now without sinking into it. A few days ago, I was reckless enough to leave my boots too close to the wall of my tent when I went to bed. The next morning, their laces were like steel rods and I had to light a fire in the middle of the day to unfreeze them. If I'd put them on while they were filled with that deadly cold, I'd have lost my toes.

My reserves of oil have diminished much faster than I expected.

My stock of wood was used up long ago. Now I burn fuel, adding the odd piece of the triangular tent that used to shelter our equipment. Every day of cold reduces my chances of survival. If I reach the bottom of the jerrycan, I will never make it off this mountain. My body heat will bleed out, little by little, and my stiff fingers will not be able to hold it in. I have not seen the sun in a week. All my hope now is in ten or fifteen litres of oil, and the sound of the liquid lapping inside the metal container haunts my dreams.

Last night I shivered inside three layers of clothing. The night was black. I am talking about that mystical blackness which is the absence of everything, not just light, the kind of night when you daren't close your eyes for fear of adding darkness to darkness. And in those hours of dread, I suddenly *heard a noise*.

The thing circled around my tent like a sigh for several minutes, the only sound that of the snow being disturbed. I was too scared to move. What could be living here? A rabbit? But the visitor took up too much air; I could perceive its mass, the place that it occupied in space, with the instinct of early man, man before fire, under constant threat, always on his guard.

I thought of a ghost. Gio's son, come to beg me for help? Peter, seeking vengeance from the depths of the glacier? All the tales and legends of my native Pyrenees haunted me, bouncing around my mind in a macabre dance. A *drac*, perhaps, that friendly donkey that our teacher warned us about, which would snatch children as they left the school, its body lengthening to let more and more of them ride on its back before taking them away to drown them in the river. In the end I cried out, like a child waking from a nightmare, and the noises stopped. I forgot about the cold and stayed up all night, watching as the walls of my canvas cocoon changed from black to khaki to emerald to lime.

Even after that, I waited. For another hour, perhaps. Finally I went out, wielding my ridiculous penknife. I was alone with my mountains, as always. But when I looked down at the snow, I saw the tracks, the furrows left behind by the beast that had circled the tent. I had not dreamed it. I shuddered with dread when I identified the author of those sinister trenches. A ghost? The idea seemed almost laughable now. I would have gladly swapped my nocturnal visitor for all the phantoms in the world. It was a wolf.

So come on then, you bearded deity, you bitter and mean old god, be honest. What did I do to you? I went to church every Sunday for years without protest, because I adored the way my mother worshipped you, praying in a whisper, my hand in hers. Because I loved feeling her tremble when you descended during the elevation – abracadabra – and when you somehow hid yourself inside the wafer-thin Host. I am no more a sinner than any other man. I have never stolen, and I have certainly never killed, and while I may have coveted my neighbour's wife occasionally, it was okay because he didn't want her any more. And as we're settling scores here, shall I tell you about all the times I found my mother in tears at the back of the barn, with a split lip or a black eye, and she begged me not to tell anyone? I could spend the whole winter telling you stories like that. So, no, don't tell me that I deserved all this – this cold, this loneliness, this pain. And now *a wolf*? You are a worse man than me, heavenly Father. And your deadly sin? I've saved that till last: you don't even exist.

My fire burns all night now. When will the animal take the hint? It is still there: I can see its tracks every morning. I doze, feeding my fire with scraps of canvas dipped in oil.

The wolf is a perfect work of nature. It watches patiently as I exhaust myself with fear. With the science of its species, it knows that a fire always goes out in the end. And I keep fighting, like so many other men before me. Instinct versus instinct.

I have never seen the animal. It prowls at the edges of the darkness, not exactly where the firelight ends, but a little further on, to hide its eyes. It is black, too: now and then I find a tuft of its fur in the snow. I have even thought, idiotically, of taming it. One night I left it some ham as an offering. The wolf didn't touch it. It prefers to wait.

My submissiveness gives way to madness. Tonight, I take my knife and I go outside and blindly slash at the dark night air with it, screaming at the wolf to come and show itself – 'if you're a man'. It does not come, obviously.

I pour out the last of the oil and stare into the empty jerrycan. Without fuel, the tent canvas won't burn. After a week of struggle, I surrender. I stir up the dying embers and retreat into the tent with my terror. Where are you, Pépin, when I need you most? The enemy will come tonight. There are too many cracks and I can't watch them all, not alone. If only my dog could curl its body around me, to protect me from harm . . .

In the early morning I wake with a start, amazed that I have slept, amazed that I am still alive. The wolf has spared me. I emerge from my tent into a morning of bright sunlight, blinded by the promise of spring. I close my eyes to filter the burning dazzle. I am as hungry as an ogre. I could eat a whole valley, trees, men, animals and all, stones cracking beneath my teeth, leaves sticking to my tongue, and wash it down with a river. I take a few steps into the snow, which sighs and creaks, squeezed under my boots like an accordion.

Alive. And then I see. There, in front of me . . . the disaster. I will not be eating any valley or men or animals. I will never eat anything again.

The trunk containing my provisions is empty. The wolf has wolfed it all down. After seven months in this combe, reduced to a shadow of myself, a poor pile of bones, hair and wiry muscles, I didn't think for a moment of hiding my Italian ham and my dried apricot somewhere safe. I thought that it was *me* the beast wanted.

Gio was right. In the mountains, it is arrogance that kills you.

The hunger began almost instantly. It's funny: I used to have to force myself to eat every day, cursing each mouthful of dried meat and its saltiness that burned my lips, cursing each piece of fruit and its sticky sweetness. Now they are all I dream of. Just let me taste them one more time, just once.

The first day, I hunted around for leftovers. I made a frozen cone with the scraps I found, and devoured it. The wolf had done a good job. It had not wasted anything or left anything behind. I imagined it in its lair, sated and sleepy, drunkenly thanking its dark and nameless gods.

The next day I ate snow. Eyes closed, I gave my sorbet exotic flavours: mango, orange blossom, perhaps a little passion fruit. I chewed on a bit of wood: mmm, what delicious liquorice! The illusion worked for a few minutes, then my stomach rebelled. I vomited up a torrent of iced water.

Today, the dish of the day is lichen. I sweep the snow from the few rocks that jut above the surface and go at them with my teeth, trying to catch anything that still survives. The rock takes more of my tooth enamel than I do its lichens, and in the end I give up. The hunger has become a physical pain, a knife stab in my guts. But none of that matters any more. Because it is now mid-February 1955 and I – Stanislas Henri Armengol, born in Tarbes in 1902 to Henri Manuel Armengol, aka the Commander, and María Dolores Jiménez, aka Mama – have just understood that I will not die from hunger.

The snow has been falling for the last hour. I had believed in the spring, I had prayed for it, but my prayers must have bounced back from the gunmetal sky. A white quilt descends, blown haywire by pizzicato gusts. I know what this means and yes, here it is, the winds' master: the great mistral with its brass howl. During the first blizzard, it attacked my curved tent; unable to find a way of lifting it from the ground, the mistral went away, furious, and plotted its revenge. This time, Gio's ingenuity cannot save me. The wind shoots through the door, left carelessly open, and grabs the canvas from the inside. The tent swells like a bubble. I am not far away. I run and manage to catch hold of a rope as it snakes through the snow. It bites my fingers through my gloves as I enter a tug of war with the mistral. It drags me through the powder snow in a furious struggle – *let go, you fool!* – but I hold tight with every ounce of my strength, ignoring the pain, refusing to surrender the wild canvas sail on which my life depends. And then finally, exhausted and defeated, I obey the wind. I let go, my fingers swollen with cold and blood.

For a long time, I lie face down in the snow. Everything burns: my skin, my breath, inside, outside. I move. Get to my knees. Crawl back to the camp. All that remains of my shelter is a circle of burned grass. I have not seen that grass in so long. The last time I saw it, it was bright and fresh, full of green dreams, but now it is white and dead.

So, no, I will not die of hunger. The cold will take me first, and I am glad about that.

The night ends. The wind blows even harder and sows the snow horizontally. I wait, my back to a rock. I am not afraid. The shivering lasted two hours. My heartbeat has slowed. Little white clouds puff from my lips like a cartoon of a toy steam train. I have no last wishes. Although I wouldn't say no to a piece of chocolate. I would also like, one last time, to feel a woman's body under my hands.

I am not afraid.

I spread my fingers in front of my eyes. The grime, the calluses, the deep lines and wounds. Which one of these lines is my lifeline? I once heard a story about an adventurer who, thinking his lifeline too short, lengthened it with a knife blade. To what end? With or without a knife, you will soon reach the end of your palm. Lengthening your lifeline — what an idea! Our hands are too small to hold anything of importance.

I'm sleepy.

Have to. Open. My eyes. *Open your eyes, Nino, you'll be late for school.* I push away Pépin, who is licking my face, his sweet puppy breath. I am not at home, I know that. I am on my mountain. For the first time, I hear it. Really hear it. The mountain is a symphony, *Bewegt, nicht ʒu schnell.* Moving, but not too fast. I always liked Bruckner.

Open your eyes. I have forgotten something. Something important.

I hear the snow, the crystals cracking. Far below, the earth is already stirring. A seed unfolds and sends a tendril up towards the surface. I hear the black rivers oozing and I sink even deeper, into the soft boiling of a volcano. Voices, music, the radio waves of the universe. Sap rising through the trunk of a tree, the splitting of an insect's egg in its cradle of moss. My prayer for spring is granted: it is not far away now. All you have to do is listen. See, Aimé? I'm listening.

I have to wake up. Something about a wolf. At the bottom of the lake, I sink softly. The ice, shattered by my weight, shines on the surface. Far away, my books float out of my school bag, and then it's the muddy bed, fear giving way to a feeling of well-being, the tall grass rising like Mama's hair when she leans down to kiss me . . . But, no, it is not my time. Hands call me. With the kick of a heel I am pulled up to the surface and I swallow an immense gulp of air.

The storm rages. I no longer feel cold. I remember. Something Gio said, long ago. *There are no wolves where we're headed . . . unless they've found a path that we don't know about.* Perhaps there is another exit, a way out of this combe other than the via ferrata.

Standing in the snow. How did I get here? Oh yes, the wolf's tracks. I have been following them for an hour. I just nodded off for a minute, leaning against a snowdrift while I gathered my strength. Beneath my feet, the tracks are still clear despite the storm. They go up the eastern side of the combe, the one I know least well. The walk has warmed me up. I've had to take off my jacket and my gloves. The sweat burns on my skin. I strip off the sweater, the woollen vest that is suffocating me. Bare-chested. Hope gives me wings; I feel no fatigue. The tracks go behind a rise in the land that creates a miniature valley on the side of the combe. A large area of snow there has been disturbed, red fur mixed with black fur. My wolf was two wolves, perhaps a couple seeking food for their young.

After the valley, the tracks continue. They go up and up, following the length of the combe, three hundred or four hundred metres above the bottom. The moon has vanished and in that instant I enter what I have learned to fear: the death of the soul, that crazy uncertainty where you even start to doubt that the sun will rise again. Don't stop, whatever you do. My shoulder brushes past a black rock that Gio pointed out to me: it's the 3,000-metre marker. The air thins and my lungs pump desperately, sucking in the little oxygen that remains.

I have been walking for two hours. And then suddenly the tracks vanish into a fresh dusting of snow halfway up the slope. A dramatic blaze engulfs the peak above me, scattering the demons that are messing with my mind, whispering the idea of wolves falling from the sky like an evil rain. Think logically, Stan. They didn't come from the sky. And if they didn't come from the sky . . .

On all fours, I sweep away the snow around me. There: a crevice in the rock! It's wide enough for me to slip inside, and I'm sleepy, so sleepy.

Not now. I am too close to give up now. *Open your eyes*. They're open; I'm being lifted out of the lake, my body laid out on the ice. Thank God the ranger happened to be passing by, somebody call for help, you okay, kid? Oh, forget all of that, it was a long time ago.

One last time, I turn to the combe. Far below, a black dot leaning against a snowdrift. It's a man, his arms around his knees: a little ball rolled under the thumb of the god of cold. Between two worlds, he resists, refuses to be crushed. That man is me. A hallucination, one of those vast dreams that Gio described.

But which one is true? Am I standing here on the slope, tracking the wolf? Or is it me down there, that crumpled man, listening to the last few beats of his heart? Which one of us is dreaming the other?

I dive into the bowels of the mountain. The path is long. I walk with my arms held out in the darkness. An endless corridor of stone, a veritable labyrinth where the wolves' tracks are visible sometimes in the grey luminescence of strange mushrooms. I stumble a thousand times. For hours and hours, again and again, until I can't any more, until . . .

A gigantic cavern. A cathedral of stalagmites. On one side, a blue stained-glass window in the middle of the wall: we are touching the glacier. On the other, the sun floods through an opening that reveals a peaceful valley. The wolves' door. Freedom. But freedom can wait.

Titanosaurus stanislasi. Leucio didn't lie. His dragon is there, in the middle of the nave, watched over by a congregation of limestone penitents. It's a diplodocus, a creature almost thirty metres long, the most perfect specimen I have ever seen. It is lying next to another one, smaller, presumably its baby. The baby is three times my size and its front feet are broken. It fell into this abyss, far back in the mists of time. Its mother fell too as she tried to rescue it. The world continued turning. Nobody mourned them because there was nobody for a long time. Because it would be another 140 million years before anyone had the idea of mourning anything. So I stay beside them, for a long time, watching over their sleep in this endless night, watching over their immense love, this love between giants.

Sleep, my dinosaurs, sleep. Soon, I will leave without waking you, because waking has been impossible for a long time.

'**I**s it for me?'

'Of course it's for you.'

Mama holds on to her suitcase. She moves forward, touches the bed – bigger than she ever imagined – and paces around her bedroom, which is located at the far end of the apartment. I open each wardrobe, one for her dresses, one for her coats, another for all the ballgowns she does not yet have.

'And look at those mouldings, Mama. Look!'

She looks at everything with her American eyes, her lips curved in a smile. She lied: she hasn't aged. She will never be old.

'Thank you, Nino. We'll be happy here together, the two of us. Just like the old days. When we had that dog that you loved so much, the grey one . . .'

'Blue. Pépin.'

'That's right! Actually, that reminds me, there's something I have to tell you about that dog . . .'

I know, Mama. I've known for a long time. Please, lie down. You've had a long trip, you must be tired. It took a lot of fossils to get to this point.

'Your poor fingernails, Nino . . . They're in a terrible state!'

Don't worry. It's my job. Put down your suitcase. Lie down and close your eyes. See, it's comfortable, isn't it? Later, we'll celebrate our reunion. We'll go to the opera, we'll dance and dance. And when you're tired, you can lean on me.

Sitting close to the bed, I listen to her breathing slow as she drifts into sleep. And now I leave, on tiptoe.

Now I turn out the light.

Spring

This is a land where quarrels last a thousand years. Nobody has come here in a long time. The old-fashioned buses lie on their sides, rusted elephants dying on the cold concrete of windswept backyards. They no longer run along the grassed-over road that leads to the abandoned village. Here, there is nothing to see, nothing to do. Nothing but ruins and sorrow.

Nobody has come in a long time, except for him. An old Italian, a giant stooped by the years, a face of stone behind thick glasses. He walks along paths opened up by the sun after a long winter. He passes empty houses, the forest under granite cliffs, crosses the log bridge, or what remains of it. He walks along the plateau, stopping only to sleep. Setting off again, he grips the mountain by its iron handles and steps over it.

When he was younger, he would make this pilgrimage every year. His visits grew more spaced out over time – that's life. But this year, 1994, is special. Special because it's the last year. Next year, he will no longer have the strength. That's life too, and it's not so bad. He's not a young man any more, as his children and grandchildren like to remind him; they tried to persuade him not to come. At eighty-seven, it's not sensible. And all for an old, old story.

He goes down into the combe on the same path. For the first time, he looks tired. He sits down for a long moment, in the place where the tents were before. A whisper of things that we cannot hear: they are for him only. He has changed in forty years: his slowness has become sublime, his patience infinite. But this place is the same. He remembers it well. He remembers everything.

The old man is about to leave when a colour catches his eye, down below. So he walks across the sky, he walks all the way to the colour. He walks beyond his age, beyond the bones that grumble and crumble and bend his giant body.

The melting snow has revealed some clothes. A jacket, a sweater, a woollen vest. They are well preserved, scattered over a path that runs along the east side of the combe. Inside the sweater is a label with the owner's name. He knows without looking that the name lacks two little letters, a suffix that only he ever pronounced. His glasses fog up – it's sweat, he thinks, rubbing at the inch-thick lenses.

Finally he turns away. He leaves without touching the jacket, the sweater, the vest. When he gets home, his wife will ask him why, from the large bed that she has not left since she fell ill. Why didn't he pick up the clothes? Umberto says he doesn't know. That he just remembers thinking, as he took one last look back:

This is the most beautiful place in the world.